RILEY

LOVING A YOUNG SERIES, BOOK 4

STACY EATON

CHAPTER ONE

RILEY

"I thought we weren't going to do this again." A gravelly voice broke the silence in the semi-dark room, and I clenched my eyes tighter as the voice throbbed through my head. Man, how much did I drink last night?

A warm hand slipped under the covers and touched my leg. "You alive over there?"

I grunted. "Barely. Why are you here, Ethan?"

"Don't tell me you don't remember? You wanted me to stay. You practically begged me to tuck you in." He rolled to his side, spooning behind me, his hand curled around my hip, his morning hard-on pressing to my backside. "You don't remember that?"

I shook my head slightly and winced.

"Bad hangover?" I nodded, and he kissed my shoulder. "Want me to make you coffee?"

I nodded again, and he kissed my shoulder once more before he let his hand rub over my hip to my bare thigh and then slide away. I managed to split my eyes wide enough to watch his naked backside as he bent down to get his boxers off the floor.

I'd have to be dead not to want to watch him naked. I closed them as he turned back to me and leaned over to kiss my brow.

"I'll be right back."

As soon as he was gone from the room, I forced myself to throw the covers back and literally rolled out of bed. On my hands and knees on the floor, I felt the room spin. My god, how much *did* I drink last night? I pulled myself off the floor and to my feet as my stomach rolled.

I managed to make it to the toilet and put my head in my hands as I used it, moaning softly. I'd gone out last night to celebrate Cinco de Mayo, and I remembered drinking a few beers, but that was normal for me. As I tried to remember what else I'd consumed, I suddenly had a memory of doing Jägermeister shots with Evan and my brother Huntley.

Damn them! I knew better than to do shots, especially on a weekday! It was hard enough recovering on the weekend. Dealing with a bunch of fourth graders was less than appealing with a pounding headache.

I stumbled to the shower, hoping the hot water would ease the pounding in my head, and tried to remember if I did beg him to stay. I couldn't recall it, but I'm sure I did—it wouldn't be the first time I had coerced Ethan into my bed. Coerced? Nah. That would imply I had forced him. Ethan always came willingly.

I sighed and pushed myself through the shower routine. Once I was done and my hair was pulled up in a messy bun, I returned to my bedroom with a towel wrapped around my body. On my dresser was a steaming cup of coffee. I scooped it up with two hands, inhaling deeply before taking a sip. Ah— perfect. I took another needed sip.

I glanced around and didn't see any of his clothing, but my bed was made. Maybe he left already. That was fine with me. It wasn't the first time we had slept with one another, although the last time was supposed to have been the *last time.*

I finished dressing, collected my phone and coffee, and went downstairs. I stopped when I entered the kitchen area. Ethan was sitting at the breakfast bar, his short hair flat on one side from sleeping, his dark-blue shirt wrinkled and untucked, and his attention on his phone.

"I thought you left."

He lifted his gaze to mine before his blue eyes skimmed my clothing. "No, I was waiting to give you a ride back to your car."

Whoops! I forgot about that. "Okay, give me a couple of minutes."

"How are you feeling?"

"I'll live." I dug around in the fridge for something to make for lunch and settled on ham and cheese. I made my sandwich, grabbed some precut veggies and bagged them, and then tossed it all into my lunchbox.

"Don't forget the dressing cup for your veggies. You want to grab breakfast on the way?"

"Oh, damn, thanks." I grabbed a single-serve dressing cup and tossed it into my bag before I glanced at the clock. "Um, I'm not sure I'll have time."

"Why don't I call in an order at Coral's, and we can grab it on the way to get your car? You can eat it at work while you read your email."

"Okay."

"You want your usual?"

"Yeah," I replied as I filled my to-go coffee mug. Ethan was just hanging up when I gathered all my stuff, and we headed out the door.

I climbed into his truck and rolled my eyes as he lifted my bra off the seat. "I think you forgot something in your rush to get me in your bed last night."

Shit! I seriously didn't even remember that. "Give me that. I'd be pissed if I lost that. It's my favorite one." I grabbed it off

3

his finger and shoved it into my tote bag, trying to hide my embarrassment.

He chuckled and started his truck as I put on my seat belt. "Do you even remember taking it off in my truck last night?"

"No."

He frowned, and I saw him glance my way after backing out of the space and putting his truck in drive. "Why am I not surprised?"

"Did I really beg you?"

"Yep, you did. You slipped out of your bra on the way home after you told me it was killing you, then when we got to your place, you climbed over the console to my lap and pleaded with me to come in."

I shook my head. "You could have said no."

He glanced at me, giving me a stern look. "I did tell you no, Ry. I reminded you that we had decided that we wouldn't sleep together anymore, but you kept saying just one more time. Come on, just one more time. You know you want to, and you know very well that I can't resist you, Riley, especially when you are rubbing that body all over mine."

I stared out the side window and pursed my lips. It sounded like something I would do. "You still could have said no."

"You are a hard woman to say no to, Riley. You know I can't resist you."

"I thought you were dating Karen," I stated.

"Kathy, and we went out a couple of times, but that didn't work out."

"Why not?"

His laugh was harsh for a second, and I glanced at him to find him shaking his head. "Same reason it never works. It just doesn't." His hand squeezed the steering wheel, and then he pulled into the small parking lot at Coral's Coffee Café and put the truck in park. "I'll be right back."

I watched him walk toward the building. His hair was still a chaotic mess, and his shirt looked like he had slept in it, but he didn't seem to care in the least. He waved at someone on the other side of the parking lot and held the door for a woman coming out with her hands full.

I sighed and rubbed my temples. We'd had a conversation a few weeks ago and had decided that we shouldn't be sleeping with one another anymore. It meant nothing to either of us—or I guess it didn't. I knew it was comfortable, easy, and well, pretty damn awesome, which sucked because I didn't want it to be awesome with him. I wanted it to be boring, so I wouldn't want to sleep with him anymore. He was practically my brother —only from different parents.

He returned a few minutes later and handed me a bag. "I got you a fruit bowl too. You always get hungry after a night of drinking around the mid-morning break."

"Thanks," I replied as he got on the road again. The silence between us was never uncomfortable, but today it felt a little tense. We pulled into the tavern's parking lot, and he parked behind my car and rested back against his seat, staring out the windshield. I knew the look. He wanted to say something, so I waited.

"Riley, we really can't do that again."

"I know," I quipped back.

He turned to look at me. "Do you? Because I seem to recall us saying this a couple of weeks ago, and I was pretty damn determined to keep my distance from you."

I shrugged and reached for the handle. "So, keep your distance, and I'll keep mine."

"I plan on it, Riley. I'm serious this time. I can't keep doing this with you. The only time you ever want to see me is when you're drunk and need a ride home and a good time. I can't remember the last time we had sex when you were sober."

I laughed. "Are you saying I have a drinking problem?"

His eyes looked serious for a moment. "Do you?"

"No!" I snapped indignantly.

"How often do you blackout when you drink, Ry? You don't even remember last night, and you didn't remember the last time either."

"Jesus, Ethan! Are you saying I'm a drunk?"

"No, I'm asking you to think about how much you drink and what happens when you do."

I snorted. "Just because I like to have fun and get a little tipsy, then have sex, doesn't mean I have a problem."

I shoved open the door as he spoke. "I didn't say you had a problem; you did, and it's never just tipsy, Riley."

I glared at him over my shoulder. "I do *not* have a problem. The only problem I have is you giving in to my every whim. It's not my fault you can't say no to me."

He frowned. "You're right. It's not your fault. It's mine, but I'm done, Riley. I can't keep doing this. I'm not going to enable you to drink more or be the guy who picks you up off the floor and takes you home for a good time because you're smashed. Not anymore."

"Then don't," I muttered as I scrambled out.

"I think you need to do some thinking, Riley."

"Who the hell do you think you are, Ethan? I'm a big girl, and I know what I'm doing."

"Do you? Because from where I am, it looks like you are kind of lost and hiding your frustration in a twelve-pack."

My jaw dropped. "Oh, my god! Just because I like to drink and have sex, you think I'm an alcoholic? You've lost your damn mind, Ethan Winston! Jesus, when did you become such a goody two-shoes?"

"No, Riley! I didn't say you were an alcoholic. I just said that you need to think about all of this, but I'm telling you that I can't keep doing this. I can't be the one that you call whenever you need a scratch itched or a ride because you have too much to drink—again. I can't do it anymore. I won't."

"Well, then, don't do it! I'm sorry I have infringed on our friendship so much. I thought that we enjoyed having sex together, and I didn't realize that getting a ride home from you was such a freaking hassle! I'll refrain from calling you in the future."

I slammed the truck door and began to dig in my tote bag. I heard the window go down on his truck. "Riley," he said sternly, and I refused to look at him. I didn't want him to see the tears in my eyes. "Riley!"

"Go away, Ethan. I think we have said all that we need to say."

He called my name roughly one more time, but I stepped away from him as I dug deeper into my tote. The jingle of keys rang through the air as they landed at my feet. I didn't even have time to pick them up before he was pulling away.

I was so furious that he would call me an alcoholic. Who was he to judge me for having a few drinks? And I got his ass to pick me up so he wouldn't yell at me later for driving under the influence. What a prick!

I snagged my keys off the ground and climbed into my SUV. I was done with him. *Done*! I didn't need him to drive me home or climb into my bed, and I sure as hell didn't need his bullshit! Ethan Winston could kiss my ass!

I frowned as I jabbed my keys into the ignition, thinking about a previous romantic interlude that I did remember, where Ethan had done just that. Whatever! I was over it. I should never have slept with him in the first place.

CHAPTER TWO

ETHAN

*T*hat damn woman! I wasn't sure how large of a sign I would have to put up to show her how I felt. Nothing would ever be big enough because she was fucking oblivious to my feelings.

A few weeks ago, I'd tried to talk to her and tell her how I felt, but she brushed my feelings aside before I could even get them out. When I hesitated, she started talking about how we shouldn't sleep together anymore, and I had agreed because I was hoping that she would realize that she missed me. That maybe she wanted to be with me for other things, and not just a good time. Sadly, she hadn't.

Last night, I told myself when I showed up at the tavern after my shift that I wasn't going to end up in bed with her. I kept my distance while she was drinking, but when it came time for me to head home, she had rubbed her sexy as hell body against my arm, given me those I want you eyes, and I hadn't been able to say no.

The whole way back to her house, while she slurred one constant word after another, I'd told myself to drop her off and leave. How could I leave her when she'd pulled her bra through her shirt sleeve and slung it around my neck, pulling me forward to kiss her? How could I go when she climbed over my lap and ground against my throbbing erection? How could I push her away when she was holding my hands to her breasts, whispering in my ear what she wanted me to do to her?

Jesus, just remembering it was giving me another major hard-on. I was stopped at a red light and slammed my fist against my steering wheel. After I'd gotten her out of my car, I'd told myself I'd walk her to her door, get her safely inside, and then I'd hightail it back to my truck. I was not going to sleep with her again.

I'd had to put her key in the door, and before I could get out of the way, she was pushing me inside, her hand pulling at my buckle and opening it way too fast—her other hand rubbing against my erection. I'd tried to turn, to push her away, but she had whipped her shirt off and thrown it into my face. Before I could remove it, she was on her knees in front of me, unzipping my pants.

And fuck if that didn't just lock my feet in place. Seeing Riley on her knees, her bare breasts jutting out, her nipples hard, and her tongue wetting her lips as she pulled me free. Yeah, that was my ultimate fantasy when it came to Riley. She gave the best fucking blow jobs—the best—and I could never deny her. Not when she was looking so eager.

She had taken me in her mouth, looking up at me with those love-me eyes, and I'd lost any thought of leaving. Instead, I'd held her head as I moved my hips back and forth, loving the way her tongue swirled around my shaft. She'd taken me to the brink of destruction with her sexy sounds as if I were giving her the ultimate gift, and not the other way around.

She always knew when I was about to lose it because she'd stop. She grinned up at me and told me in that sexy as hell bedroom voice, "Not yet, baby." I had scooped her into my arms and kissed her like I was a man about to starve, and she was my only sustenance.

The bad thing was, she kind of was. I'd know for a long time that I was in love with Riley Young, but she never acted as if she felt the same.

I'd carried her to her room. Riley squirmed, and the minute her feet were on the floor, she was tugging my pants off my hips as I tried to get hers off too. When Riley had been drinking, she was a wild one in bed. She liked it a little rougher, a little wilder. She talked more, begged for me to please her, or give her more of something, and last night had been no different.

Riley didn't have to beg, though. I would give her anything that she asked for—well, I had in the past. I had to put my foot down and cut the cord to Riley. She didn't want me as a man to build a life with. She wanted me to hit all the right buttons and have her writhing in ecstasy under my mouth.

I growled to myself as I pulled into my driveway. I could practically taste her on my tongue now. I knew her so well— from the taste of the salty skin on her neck when she was sweaty, to the erotic scent of her during lovemaking. I knew it— I craved it.

I had to fucking stop. Was there a twelve-step program to rid Riley Young from my life?

I went straight to my shower, ripping my clothes off as I did, and turned the water on hot. I fisted my erection, cursing it for wanting her so badly, and then I thought back on our night one last time as I stroked myself.

The orgasm was harsh, almost painful, as it finally hit me, and I leaned against the tile wall, staring at the drain. I needed to let all my dreams go. Let all of my fantasies of her go and wash them right down the sewer pipe. It was time to be done with that stupid dream.

I finished showering and went to make breakfast since I'd sent my sandwich with her. As I ate, my phone rang, and I paused in chewing as I looked at the screen and then swallowed as fast as I could.

"Hello?" I answered, my stomach instantly twisting nervously. I'd been waiting for this call. Was it going to be good or bad? Holy crap, my heart had started to race.

"Ethan? It's Scott Hendricks down at the County Detectives Office."

"Detective Hendricks, how are you?"

"I am doing well, and I told you before to call me Scott."

"Alright, Scott it is."

His hesitation was only a few seconds, and I closed my eyes as I waited. "So, I'm calling to see if you are still interested in the county detective position."

My eyes flashed open. "Are you serious?"

"I sure am."

"Holy crap! Yes! Yes, I'm interested. Of course, I'm interested."

He chuckled over my enthusiasm. "Fantastic. I think you are going to fit in great with our group. Everyone here knows you, and many have already worked with you. None of them have had bad things to say. Trust me—I tried to find something." We both laughed.

"I'm glad to hear that, Scott."

"So, you tell me when you might be able to start."

"Well, I'm going to need to give my notice. I actually have a lot going on in the next few weeks. Hold on a second; let me look at my calendar on my phone."

"Sure, take your time."

I brought it up quickly and skimmed over my work schedule. "Scott, I could start on the twenty-sixth. Would that work for you?"

"That would actually work out well."

"Okay, then I better get my notice in."

"Great idea." He paused. "I have another question for you. There is a training course that is coming up. You literally would start with us on the twenty-sixth, and then on the sixth of June, we'd need you to travel. It's a pretty intense training, but we really need someone to take this."

"What's it for?"

"Polygraph."

Whoa! Was he serious? Polygraph? I'd never pictured myself doing that. "Isn't that training like two months?"

"Actually, it's twelve weeks, and you'd have to head to Georgia for that time. Think you can do that? Any interest?"

"Do you think I'd be any good at it?"

He chuckled. "If we didn't think you could handle it, we wouldn't have hired you for the position here. We know that you will be able to handle everything that comes your way. You also have a very calm nature, and you're a pretty likable guy, so that will work for you with being a polygrapher."

"Well, thank you for that vote of confidence. Can I think about that for a day?"

He chuckled. "Yeah, I guess I did throw a lot at you all of a sudden. Charlie retires later this year; he's the only one that we have certified in polygraphy, and Brad was supposed to go to this class, but his wife is pregnant and just got put on bed rest, so he can't leave her that long."

"I'm interested. I just—I just need to digest this. I'll get back to you by tomorrow. I'm pretty sure it's going to be a yes—like ninety percent sure—but let me roll it around in my mind. My head is kind of spinning."

"Absolutely, you got it. Let me know, and we look forward to having you onboard either way."

"Thanks again, Scott. I'm excited to be joining you all."

He told me he was sending me some paperwork and to look

it all over and get it back to him. The moment we hung up, I dialed my father.

"Morning, Ethan. Your mom wants to know if you're going to make it this weekend."

I hesitated. This weekend? Oh, yeah, Coral's birthday. "Yeah, I'll be there. Are we celebrating Mother's Day too?"

"No, your momma wants to have a small brunch with you all on Sunday. Your sisters are already planning the menu."

"Okay, tell them to let me know if they need anything."

"Great, I will. How are you?" he asked, and I heard the squeaking of the back door as it closed.

"I got the position." The words exploded from my mouth.

"You got the position?" he asked quietly, and then it must have dawned on him what I was saying. "Oh, you got the job!"

"Yeah, Dad. I just hung up with Detective Hendricks."

"Ethan, that's fantastic. Your mom is going to be so proud of you. Who else have you told?"

"No one. You were the first person I called. I literally just hung up with him."

"Of course, I was. You are going to accept it, right?"

"No doubt. I have wanted to be a detective since I was in college. But get this, they want to send me to polygraph school as soon as I start."

"Polygraph school?"

"Yeah." I explained why I'd been offered the spot. "But I'd have to go to Georgia for twelve weeks."

"Wow, what an opportunity, Ethan. Are you going to do it?"

"I have to think it over a little more, but I'm pretty sure that I'm going to do it."

"Son, you have worked hard all your life, especially going through this process. I think this would be fantastic for you."

"Thanks, Dad. I really appreciate that."

"Well, how about we announce it at your sister's birthday?"

14

"Ah, I wouldn't want to do that. It's Coral's day. I don't want to distract from her birthday."

"You know that she will be so excited. Everyone will. I can't believe my son is going to be a county detective. I'm so proud of you, Ethan."

"Thanks, Dad. I'm really excited about it. Maybe we can announce it at the end of the party."

"I assume you already took the job."

"I did."

"And when would you go to this class that they want you to take?"

"June sixth, I believe is what he said. It's a twelve-week course."

"Whew, that's a long time. Do you get to come home at all during that time?"

"I really don't know. I'm not even sure I want to do it."

Suddenly, the thought of not seeing Riley for twelve weeks hit me, and I leaned back in my seat. Maybe this was exactly what I needed to do to get her out of my mind. Three months of distance would be enough to put my feelings behind me, wouldn't it?

Yes!

I laughed. "I think I just officially made my decision, Dad."

"Well, that was fast." My father chuckled. "What made you decide so quickly?"

"Nothing really. I just remembered how hard I worked to get this. I want to do something important in my life. This training would put me in a good place within their department."

"It sounds like it sure would. I'll let your momma know."

"Tell her not to share it with anyone until this weekend. Let's wait until Coral's party is winding down, then I will announce it."

"Sounds like a fantastic idea."

As I finished my breakfast, I glanced at a picture on the side-wall. Riley was in it, of course, but so were my siblings: Evan, Coral, Candy, Carmen, Cara; and hers: Huntley, Henley, Wesley, Bradley, and Kayley.

I stared at the picture for a minute. We were all close, had grown up together, argued as one big happy family. Bradley and Cara had dated in middle school. Candy and Wesley dated briefly in high school. Despite those blips on growing up, we'd all remained close.

Especially Riley and me. I was best friends with her Irish twin, Henley, and we hung out together all the time. Henley and I used to keep her out of trouble, and then Henley got tired of his sister and moved on to women not related to him. I'd been fascinated with Riley since I was sixteen. Half of my freaking life, I'd been in love with a woman who didn't even care I was alive.

I was done. It was time to let Riley go and move on with my life. She could find someone else to pick her drunk ass up off the floor or someone to scratch her sexual itches.

That thought brought me up short, but then, I realized that was just one more thing I had to get over. No jealousy allowed. That was a wasted emotion.

With that decided, I logged on to my laptop and started reading over the paperwork that Scott sent me. I had papers to sign to accept the position, tax forms to complete, confidentiality forms to fill out, and that was just for the job. He also slipped in the packet of information on the polygraph class. I chuckled when I saw it. It included all the registration forms, plus what to expect, what to bring, and what to do to prepare before I arrived.

My phone rang, and I saw it was Henley. "Hey, man. How are you?"

"I'm good. How was my sister this morning?"

"I don't know. I dropped her off last night."

Henley laughed. "No, you didn't. I saw your truck there this morning. Do you honestly think I don't know you two are seeing each other?"

I winced. The parking lot at her complex had been packed last night, and I'd had to park in a different spot. "Wait, hold on. We are *not* seeing each other. Riley and I are most definitely *not* seeing each other."

"So, you just slept with my sister because she was drunk," he said, and I didn't reply. "Or do you two do this often while you're *not* seeing each other?"

"Lee, you know that I care about your sister."

"Yeah, you've been in love with her since we were kids. I was hoping that you two were finally going to get together."

"That's not happening."

"Says who? You? Or Her?"

I sighed. "It's mutual." I didn't want to throw her under the bus. "Besides, I'm gonna be out of town for a while."

"What, you going on vacation?" He laughed.

"No, I got the county detective position, and they are sending me away to polygraph school."

"No shit?"

"Yeah, I just found out an hour ago."

"Ethan, that's awesome! Man, I know you have been working on that process for a while. Shit, you were talking about doing it ten years ago. I'm glad you did. Damn, my boy's gonna be a county dick. Who else knows?"

I chuckled. "Only my parents. I haven't said anything to anyone else yet."

"Not even Riley?"

"Why would I tell your sister?"

"Because you love her. How long is the polygraph class?"

"Twelve weeks, and it's in Georgia."

"Wow. That's a long training. When are you going to tell Ry?"

I blurted out a laugh. "She'll find out this weekend with everyone else."

"Oh, man, that is gonna be fun! You are crazy, but okay. Can't wait to see how she reacts." He laughed heartily, and for just a second, I wondered if maybe she would react to the news.

It didn't matter what she did, though. I was leaving in a month, and I'd be gone for twelve weeks. I just needed to keep my distance for the next four weeks. Then by the time I got back, hopefully, I would be over Riley.

CHAPTER THREE

RILEY

*a*s soon as I got to my classroom, I dug around in my locked file cabinet for my Tylenol and popped two. Then I opened most of the blinds, picked up a drawing that had fallen to the floor, and sat down at my desk. I'd eat my breakfast while I looked over my email.

The parents of my fourth graders were a bit needy. Not as bad as when I taught second grade, but they were still needy enough that they reached out quite often with concerns. I didn't mind. Most of the time, I appreciated the heads-up or the comments they gave me. Of course, a few parents needed more handholding than their children, but I was also used to that.

I pulled open the bag containing my breakfast and removed two sandwiches and a bowl of mixed fruit, but not just any mixed fruit. This one was specifically made for me because it didn't have any pineapple in it. I hated pineapple. I set the fruit to the side and looked at the two sandwiches.

One was a plain bagel, and the other was whole wheat. Both contained two eggs and cheese, but the whole wheat one had turkey bacon, while the other had regular bacon—and extra.

Man, I loved bacon. I sighed as I set his healthier sandwich to the side and unwrapped mine.

In the past, I would have sent him a message about how his sandwich was so good, but not today. I was still pissed at him for insinuating that I had a drinking problem. I didn't. Who was he to say that I did? What was wrong with me for having a good time? I knew many people who enjoyed going out and drinking, and yes, I did enjoy sex when I was drinking. Of course, sex with Ethan anytime was pretty spectacular, but when I had been drinking, I was able to let down my hair—so to speak. I wasn't embarrassed to ask for what I wanted—wasn't afraid to experiment, and he sure loved to experiment.

I took a bite and thought for a moment. When was the last time that Ethan and I had sex and I hadn't been drinking? I frowned. Damn, I wasn't sure I even knew.

I stared at his sandwich and then tossed it into the trash—no more Ethan. I needed to stop thinking about him. I tried to read one of my emails but got stuck on a memory from last night. I'd gotten Ethan inside my place, and I'd dropped to my knees.

I'd never been a fan of going down on a man, but with Ethan, there wasn't anything I didn't enjoy. Especially as he was always neatly manscaped, oh snap, did I hate a man who didn't neaten up his package!

Maybe I was a little selfish when it came to sex. Okay, I was a lot selfish. I preferred to be pleased, not doing the pleasing. Most times, it was easy. I loved the power I held over men. I wasn't sure what it was about me, but I never did have trouble finding a date. I knew I was pretty, but I wasn't drop-dead gorgeous. I think most of the guys said I was fun, so maybe that was why.

I sighed around the food in my mouth. Dates were easy, but dates with someone worth seeing more than a couple of times were few and far between. I couldn't remember the last guy I'd gone out with more than three times. Especially one that I had sex with *and* went out with three times. Usually, after the second date, I'd know that they weren't right. By the end of the third date, I was already on to the next guy.

I was great at letting guys down easy. Most of them wouldn't even hesitate to go out with me again if I called out of the blue, but I never did.

A new email popped into my mailbox, and I smiled as I clicked it open. It was from Joseph Newman. He and his kids had moved to town two months ago. His son, Chip, was a cutie. Very intelligent and observant, but emotionally reserved and quiet. I knew that it probably had to do with the death of his mother last year. I read the email as I sipped my coffee.

Ms. Young, I hope you are doing well. I was wondering if you might be available after school for a short conference. I wanted to speak with you about something, but it would be much easier to do in person. If you are available, please let me know what time would work for you. Thank you, Joe Newman

Hmm, I wonder what that was about? I had spoken with Mr. Newman several times via email since Chip joined my class, but I had never met him in person. Jo Beth, one of our guidance counselors, said he was gorgeous, but she was also a cat person, so who knew if her taste in men matched mine.

I typed a note back to Mr. Newman that I would be more than happy to meet with him around four if that would work for him. School got out at three-forty, so that would allow me to get the room back in order before he arrived. The kids would be working on science projects this afternoon, and I did not doubt that the place would be a mess.

My personal life might be a disaster, but my classroom never was. I loved teaching children, which was weird since I didn't particularly want any of my own. Maybe one day, but that would require me to find a man I wanted to spend time with— like a lifetime of time—or at least eighteen years. I couldn't imagine being with someone that long. My parents had been together for over forty. People didn't do that anymore, and with my track record, I knew it would never happen. I'd be lucky to get four years with someone.

I fretted as I finished my breakfast. I was totally jealous of my three brothers. Okay, well, all four of them. Bradley might not be married right now, but he had been. It wasn't his fault that his wife had passed away from cancer. If she hadn't been sick, I bet they would have been married for forty years like Mom and Dad.

I did not doubt that Wes and Charlotte would stay married forever, and now that Roxy and Henley had tied the knot, I had a feeling they would be too. Now, Hunt and Dani, well, they had just gotten back together, so we'd see what happened with those two. Kayley and I were the last two. Strange that all the men in our family had fallen in love, and us two ladies hadn't. I wonder if Kay ever thought about that. I'd have to ask her next time she was home.

A few high-pitched voices echoed down the hallway, and laughter filtered in my door. I glanced at the clock. The first bus was here, and the kids would be filling the halls and the class-rooms soon. My headache was easing up, and I hadn't thrown up my breakfast. That was all good.

It was time to put aside thoughts of finding love and focus on the little people that I adored more than any grown-up I knew—well, except my parents. Okay, and maybe my siblings. Damn—and Ethan. No, scratch that—not Ethan.

I LOVED MY KIDS, all twenty-one of them—most days. Today, it was like every single one of them had been amped up on a 16-ounce coffee with extra sugar. Holy smokes! I was scrubbing one of the worktables to get the food coloring off the surface from our science project, wondering why I had ever become a teacher in the first place, when there was a knock behind me.

"Ms. Young?" a deep voice cut through the quiet, and I spun around, quickly glancing at the wall clock over his head to see it was a couple of minutes before four.

"Mr. Newman?" I set down my cleaning supplies and approached him, taking inventory of the handsome man in front of me. Well, well. Jo Beth and I could both agree on something. The man was gorgeous with his chocolate-brown hair and bright-hazel eyes. His smile was eager, and his teeth were white and straight. I sure did love a man who smiled with his whole mouth, and not a raised lip like he was smirking. Ethan smiled with his entire mouth.

Nope! Do *not* compare this man to Ethan.

Mr. Newman stepped into my room, running his eyes down to my feet and back up, looking surprised as he did. I held my hand out, and he took it, bringing his eyes back to my face. "Wow, Chip said you were pretty, but—um—yeah—sorry about that." He pulled his hand away, his cheeks turning a bit pink. Holy cow, was he blushing? I don't think I'd seen a grown man blush in years.

"Well, that was very kind of him." I gave him my sweetest smile. "It is very nice to meet you in person, Mr. Newman."

"It's Joe. Please call me Joe."

"Of course, and my first name is Riley."

He repeated my name, and I found myself rather intrigued by the man in front of me. He really was a handsome man. We continued to stare at one another for a few more moments, and a set of children's feet running down the hallway brought me back to reality.

"I'm sorry, where are my manners? Please, have a seat. What was it that you wanted to talk to me about?"

The two of us settled into seats at the table. While they weren't child-sized, they were smaller than adult chairs, and I suddenly felt like Alice in Wonderland as I continued to stare at Joe.

"I appreciate you seeing me on such short notice."

"I try to make myself available for the parents whenever they need to speak to me."

"Chip really enjoys having you as his teacher. It's been rough moving here, but he seems to be doing pretty well."

"He has a sister, doesn't he?" I asked, remembering Chip mentioning someone but not recalling the name.

"Yes, Sasha. She's in Mrs. Elmer's class."

"She's a sweet lady."

"Sasha really likes her too."

It was apparent that this man adored his children. His eyes sparkled, and his voice sounded happy. "That's good to hear. So, what can I do to help?"

The loving expression on his face shifted, and the sparkle that had been in his eyes slightly diminished. "Sasha's birthday is in two weeks, and we are starting to plan it."

"Okay," I replied, not understand why that would be a problem. Birthdays for kids were always exciting.

"Sasha and her mother shared the same birthday. This year is going to be rough since it's the first one we have celebrated since Suzanne died."

I didn't even hesitate as I reached out and touched his arm. "I'm so sorry about your wife, Joe. I can't even imagine what you are going through. My brother has two children, and his wife passed from cancer a couple of years ago. I see what he goes through every day, and I am in awe of how he keeps it all together."

"It's hard some days. There are times when I just want to throw my hands in the air, grab a bottle of tequila, and say screw it." He chuckled for a moment.

I gave him an understanding smile. "I can imagine. What can I do to help?"

"Nothing really, except if you'd keep an eye on Chip. He's quieter these days, and I'm not sure if the anniversary is going to bother him or not. I don't know what to expect."

"Has he had a tough time with her death?"

"Yeah, some days are super hard for him. He saw it happen. He was waiting outside for Suzanne to finish her run. She had just turned onto our road, and he watched a car race around the corner and hit her. The driver struck Suzanne, but after she landed, he ran over her and kept on going. Chip saw the whole thing, and he ran to her and saw the carnage left. It was not a pretty sight."

My hand had flown to my mouth. "Oh, my god! That's awful!"

"Yes, it was. It's the reason we moved. We had to get away from that street, had to get *him* away from those memories. I would find Chip standing in the front yard staring at the corner sometimes."

"Oh, I can completely understand!" I thought for a moment. "You know, this makes a lot of sense now. Chip has said a few things that didn't quite make sense, but now they do. Nothing major, just random comments at times that told me there was a story there."

He nodded as he glanced around the room. "Yeah, well, I should have told you the story sooner."

"I'm glad that we finally had a chance to talk. I'll keep an eye on him, and if I see anything here in class, I'll let you know. Is he in therapy?"

"He was, but after we moved, he seemed to be doing so much better, and he hasn't seemed to need to talk to anyone."

"Well, if you find out that he does, I know a really good child psychologist."

"I appreciate that, Riley."

"Anything I can do," I replied as our eyes locked again, and I wanted to stress that comment—anything!

CHAPTER FOUR

ETHAN

*M*y chief had been aware of my application to the County Detectives Office, so when I went into his office later that morning, he wasn't all that surprised. He stated that as much as he hoped I would succeed, he'd had his fingers crossed that someone else would get the job. He hated losing me, but he knew that at least he'd have someone he could depend on at the county level when major cases came in.

In a small town, word traveled fast, and I didn't want my family to hear about my new job before I got a chance to announce it this weekend. Henley was the only person that I had spoken with about it, besides my father, so I asked the chief to keep it under wraps for a few days.

He wished me well and told me that I would always have a place here if I changed my mind.

What was Riley going to say? Would she wish me well? The chances are that I'd probably move closer to our county seat so that I'd be closer to our office. As it was, Millerstown was on the very edge of our county. Would she care? Did I want her to? Perhaps I wanted her to beg me not to leave, just like she did when I brought her home. Would she ask me to stay closer? If she did, would I?

Nope! I was done with Riley and her wicked, sexy ways. She was no good for me, and I needed to get over her and move on. I looked forward to putting that distance between us and focusing on something else. Something that did not have anything to do with her.

So, if that was what I wanted, why, as I drove to my parents' house on Saturday, was I a nervous wreck about saying anything at the end of Coral's party? I knew that everyone would be happy for me, and I was excited about it. All of them, including Riley, knew I had applied. It wasn't like I could hide it. The process had included many of them during interviews on my background check.

I hadn't seen Riley since I dropped her off at her car Thursday morning. Usually, we texted a few times a day, and I'd found myself a few times pulling up her contact information to do just that. Only to shake my head at myself and ditch the message I was going to write.

She hadn't contacted me either, and I knew she was still pissed at me for what I said. Did I feel bad about that? Not really. She did drink a lot, and recently, she'd been drinking enough to have blackout spells. I think I had only one or two episodes like that in my thirty-two years, and they were minor. The first being my twenty-first birthday, and the next was when I'd graduated from the police academy and had gotten a job.

I had no intention of ever doing that again and had a hard time accepting that she liked to do that or that she would drink so much over and over again that it would continue to happen.

I pursed my lips as I turned the corner. I hadn't meant to call her an alcoholic, but wasn't her behavior just that? A person who wasn't able to control their urges to drink, drank enough to have blackout spells, and didn't see the effect they were having on themselves or others? I was pretty sure that was the exact description of being an alcoholic.

I knew her denial was also precisely that of someone with a drinking problem. God knew that I'd seen my share of them on the job. Maybe I needed to say something to Henley about it. Perhaps he could talk some sense into his sister, or maybe he would tell me to go pound sand and that his sister didn't have a problem.

I sighed as I pulled down the lane to my parents' house and parked. I was about an hour late, but that was okay. I'd had to help out with a situation at work for a few hours, and I knew that my family would now be just about ready to eat.

There were quite a few cars here already, and as my eyes slipped over each of them, I didn't see Riley's SUV. Okay, maybe she wasn't coming. That was probably better.

It was a beautiful May evening, and kids were out in the side yard kicking a soccer ball. Music was playing around back, and little lights were strung along the bushes of the pathway. Laughter and voices pulled me forward, and I ran into Wesley as I rounded the house.

"Hey, there you are. I was wondering if you were going to make it."

"Yeah, I had to go into work for a little while." I slapped him on the back as Marisol ran past me.

"Hi, Uncle Ethan," she called out merrily as she raced toward the other kids.

"Hey, Marisol." Wes's eyes followed her as she ran, and a smile slipped over his lips. "You really love that little girl, don't you?"

"Oh, man. That young lady had me wrapped around her finger the day she fell off the jungle gym."

I laughed, remembering the story of how he'd been jogging and seen her fall. Her mother, Charlotte, had attacked him for putting his hands on her to check her. Charlotte had later learned in the ER that Wes was a doctor and not a creeper.

"When are you gonna settle down and have a few of your own?" Wes asked as he peered my way.

I laughed again. "Yeah, well, I think that all depends on when I find a woman that wants the same thing that I do."

Wesley frowned slightly and looked off to the side. I followed his gaze to where it landed on Riley as he spoke. "Yeah, I guess she hasn't grown up yet."

"Ha! Yeah, I'm not sure your sister will ever grow up," I said as Riley sipped from a beer and leaned toward a man that I didn't know. "Who is she with?"

"His name is Joe Newman; that's all I know. He's new to the area, I think."

He was laughing at something that she said. He seemed enthralled with her, but weren't most men? I shifted my gaze off him to find her looking at me. For two seconds we stared at one another, and I knew that she was still mad at me. She turned away, leaning closer to the guy and putting on her flirt.

"I'm going to go find a beer," I said to Wes as I slapped his shoulder and went to find the cooler. On my way, I stopped and said hello to people I passed, and it wasn't until almost two hours later that my path finally crossed with Riley and her date. Until then, I'd been able to keep my distance. It was easy to be conversing on the opposite side of the yard with forty people here.

I removed a beer from the cooler and looked up to see the guy waiting to get one. "You need one—or two?"

"Oh, just one, thanks." I collected a bottle for him and passed it over."We haven't met. I'm Ethan Winston. You're here with Riley, right?"

"Yeah." We shook, and I appreciated his firm and businesslike grip. "Joe Newman."

As if saying her name brought her to us, she stepped next to

Joe and retrieved the beer bottle from him as she cozied up to his side. His eyes locked on her face, and he casually put his hand to her lower back as she faced me.

"Ethan."

"Riley," I replied.

"I see you met Joe."

"I did, and I see the beer is for you." Her eyes popped wide for a moment before she narrowed them at me.

"Rude, even for you, Officer Winston."

I shook my head and laughed before I turned back to her date. "It was nice to meet you, Joe. Good luck with this one, and just a word of advice, cut her off after six. After that, she starts doing shots, and that's not so pretty."

Riley's jaw dropped, and Joe spiked a brow, but I didn't care what either of them thought as I walked away. I actively made sure to keep my distance and my back to them. After the cake was cut and distributed, my father pulled me up to the deck.

"Hey, can I have everyone's attention? I have some news that I want to share with everyone, and I know Coral is not going to mind at all sharing the spotlight with this one." People turned their attention toward us, and I scanned the backyard, taking in all of our friends and family. My gaze paused on Riley but then kept going. I wasn't sure if she was a friend or family anymore.

I was a little surprised that I had said that to her and her date. It wasn't like me to be catty or rude. Unfortunately, my defense mechanism was kicking in to keep her further than arm's length until I could put more distance between us. That training class was going to be a godsend and couldn't come soon enough.

My father pulled me closer to his side, putting an arm around my shoulders. "You all know that Ethan takes his job very seriously, and he has served this community well for almost ten years now. What you might not know is that Ethan has always had higher dreams."

My eyes slipped back to Riley, and I watched her as my father spoke. One of her brows popped up, but otherwise, nothing.

"Now, one of those higher dreams is about to come true. His mother and I are so proud to announce that Ethan is now a County Detective—or will officially be in a couple of weeks. And not only that, but they are sending him to Georgia for three months to get certified as a polygrapher! Isn't that cool? No more lying to Ethan; he'll make you do a polygraph."

"Are you serious?" my sister Cara thundered from my left, but I couldn't look toward her. I was absorbing the expression on Riley's face.

She stared back at me, her lips parted in surprise, her brow lined momentarily, and then she turned and faced away as if she were trying to school her features. When she shifted my direction again, I saw I was right. Her facial expressions were blank.

I tore my eyes from her and knew that somewhere inside of me, I was secretly pleased with her surprise. I accepted congratulations and hugs and answered many questions after apologizing to Coral for pulling the attention off of her.

"Oh, please! We have birthdays every year. How often do you get a county detective job? I'm so thrilled for you. What does Riley think?"

I frowned. "What does she have to do with this?"

Coral's gaze cut off to the side as her jaw dropped. "You didn't tell her before tonight, did you?"

"Why would I?"

She rolled her eyes. "Oh, come on, Ethan. Everyone at this party knows that you're in love with her, and she loves you too."

"Ha! I don't think her date would like that information." I laughed loudly, "And that is most definitely not true."

"What, the part about you loving her or her loving you?"

"Either!" I joked back but was slightly irritated that we were talking about this. "Look, I gotta go talk to a few more people. Happy birthday, Coral. I love you."

"I love you, too, Ethan, and you can avoid the subject all you want. You can't get away from it."

"Yeah, actually, I can, for at least three months." I winked at her and disappeared into the crowd. I spoke to a few more people before I walked off to the side and watched the kids playing with glow sticks in the side yard.

"How long have you known?" A voice reached out to me from behind. I didn't bother to turn around.

"I got the acceptance on Thursday."

"Why didn't you tell me?"

I turned to her then. "You just learned about it with everyone else. I told exactly three people before tonight. Why would I share something like that with you anyway, Riley?"

"Why?" Her voice rose. "Because we are friends, Ethan."

"Friends? Is that all we are?" I stepped closer to her, needing to suddenly know if there was a reason for me not to push her away.

She stared at me. "Of course we are friends, Eth—"

"But is that all we are? Do you have any other feelings for me, Riley?"

"What?" She shuffled back slightly. "Why would I have feelings for you, Ethan?"

"Maybe because you love me. Maybe because we've been sleeping together on and off for *six fucking* years, and I know every little thing about you."

She gasped and then hissed as she leaned forward. "You don't know a damn thing about me!"

"I don't? That's funny, Riley, because I'm pretty damn sure I do. I know exactly how much cream is too much in your coffee and that you want mayo on one side of your ham and cheese sandwich and mustard on the other, and no, they can't mix. I know that you prefer to do laundry on Monday nights and that when you are alone, you fall asleep to the sound of waves on your sound machine." I shifted forward, reaching behind her and tugging her long hair to expose her neck as I leaned forward and put my mouth next to her ear. "I know that you love to suck me off and no other man and that you like to have your hands tied when you're drunk, but you only trust me to do it. I know you will orgasm three times with me. Every. Time. We. Have. Sex. Twice when my mouth is between your legs."

Her breath sucked in, and I pulled back, letting her hair go. "I know you always lose your car keys, and while that black bra is your favorite, it's also the most uncomfortable one that you wear. You line your damn shoes up perfectly, but you can't take the time to hang up your jackets. Your bed is made every morning, and the sheet has to be folded over the comforter exactly two inches near the pillow. It takes you nine minutes to shower unless you are hungover, and then it takes fifteen. I know that after you drink six beers, you like to switch to shots—but only tequila or rum, bourbon or whiskey give you a migraine, and that after you do four of those, you black out and won't remember a damn thing. Do you want me to keep going, Riley, because I can! I know a million things about you."

She pushed at my chest. "You don't know anything, Ethan. Go play with your stupid detective friends and stay out of my life."

"Gladly!" I started to step around her, and she grabbed my arm to stop me. It was right then that we both saw Joe watching us from only a few feet away. I did not doubt that he had heard every word—even the private ones. I shrugged out of her hold and muttered to Joe as I passed. "Good luck with her. She's a fucking hot mess."

CHAPTER FIVE

RILEY

*T*he day that Joe Newman came to see me, we had ran into each other again as I left the building. We chatted about how his other conference went as we headed toward the parking lot, and then we had paused beside his car in the visitor spot.

"This might seem very forward of me, or inappropriate, so please tell me if it is, but I was wondering if maybe you'd be interested in going out sometime. I mean, if you're allowed to date a student's parent."

"Well, we don't have any specific restrictions against it, but I do have to remain unbiased to the student. I can't give them special treatment if I am dating their father."

"So, is that a yes?"

I nodded with a smile. "That's a yes."

"Are you busy Friday night?"

"I am busy Friday, but I have a birthday party to go to on Saturday. I'd love for you to come as my plus one or plus three. You could bring the kids if you'd like. There will be other children there."

"Whose birthday?"

"Coral Winston. She owns the coffee café in town. Our family and hers are very close, and we always celebrate our birthdays together."

He hesitated. "Let me think about that. I'm not sure if the kids are ready for me to date yet, but that might make for a nice outing."

I opened my phone and brought up my contacts. "Here, put your number in here, and I'll text you mine. You can let me know later in the week."

He typed in his number and handed the phone back. I sent him a quick message, *hello handsome*, and he glanced at his phone and grinned. "Got it."

"Okay, well, don't be a stranger, and have a good evening," I said as I sauntered backward.

My day might have started rough, but it sure was ending on a pleasant note.

JOE HAD DECIDED to leave the kids at home, as he wasn't ready to introduce them to a relationship. I was glad that it was only the two of us, and I enjoyed our time together.

For the last few days, Joe and I had been texting on and off. It was fun, and he seemed like a great guy. Hadn't I said that we needed new blood in this town? It looks like we had it, and I was lucky enough to get to check it out first. I knew that because he told me that I was the first one he had dated since his wife's death. With that knowledge, I knew we needed to take it slow and wait until he was ready for more—if that's what I wanted.

I hadn't heard from Ethan, and that was just as well because I was still pissed off at him for what he'd said. I was not an alcoholic, and he had no right to say that I was.

I knew the moment he arrived at the party and was irritated that I was so aware of him. I pretended that I didn't realize he was there and focused on my date. He seemed to appreciate my flirting, and the two of us had decent chemistry.

When I saw Ethan and Joe talking, I approached them quickly, wondering if I'd come up in the conversation. Not that I cared if they spoke about me, but I wanted to make sure that Ethan didn't go bad-mouthing me to my date.

Lucky for us both, he kept his mouth shut—mostly. It was as his father shared the news that I felt my reality shift slightly. Ethan was leaving our small police department. Ethan couldn't leave—I mean, he could, but he couldn't! Millerstown was his home. He had a good job here. He didn't need another one across the county. Tears began to fill my eyes, and I turned abruptly to get control over myself again.

Shortly after I was back in control, I started to get angry. How could Ethan not have said anything to me? I had to speak with him, find out why he was doing this.

I finally saw my opportunity and slipped away from Joe as he spoke with Carmen about kids and treatment, and I approached Ethan from behind. "How long have you known?"

He didn't even turn around. "I got the call on Thursday."

I was shocked that he had only told a couple of people. A week ago, I would have been on that shortlist, but after our fight Thursday morning, I'd been struck from it.

Ethan got in my face, and my heart raced. My emotions were running on hyperspeed as I listened to him. We were friends—only friends. The things he knew were trivial—and sexy, and I hated that he did know all these things about me.

I pushed him away. "You don't know anything, Ethan. Go play with your stupid detective friends and stay out of my life."

"Gladly!" He shifted to walk around me, and my heart suddenly ached. We couldn't end things this way, and I grabbed his arm to stop him. We had to talk about this. I needed Ethan!

Except as I reached for him, I saw a very surprised Joe watching us off to the side. Oh, shit! How much had he heard?

I heard Ethan mumble something as he passed Joe, but I had no idea what it was. The blood was pounding in my ears as I glared at Ethan's back for a minute and fumed.

"I'm so sorry you had to walk in on that." I finally broke the awkward silence between us as I approached Joe.

"I apologize for interrupting." He was observing me cautiously. "You okay?"

"Yeah." I waved a hand in the air. "I'm fine. Ethan and I have a complicated past. I guess he's upset because he cares about me in a way that I don't care for him."

"But you were sleeping with him?"

"I did, but not anymore. Ethan is old news." I put my hand on Joe's arm. "I truly am sorry you had to hear that."

"It's okay. I guess we both have pasts. Hell, my past comes with ghosts and two kids, so I can't say much about yours." He chuckled slightly and then grew serious. "Just tell me one thing."

I cocked my head. "Okay?"

"Is it really over between you two? I mean, I don't want to get in the way of anything. I like you, Riley, but I don't want to come between two people if they are just having a moment. I can't afford to do that with being a single father."

I stepped closer to him, taking Joe's face in my hands. "Ethan is old news. Whatever we might have had in the past is very over. I like you too, Joe. I'd like to see what happens between us."

His hands landed on my hips. "I'm glad, Riley. Can I tell you that I've been dying to do this all night?" He leaned forward and kissed me slowly. It was a nice kiss—it didn't make me burn or anything—but it was pleasant and held promise.

"What did he say to you as he left?"

Joe chuckled. "He told me good luck because you were a hot mess."

I ground my teeth, and Joe rubbed his knuckles down my cheek. "Don't worry about it. I do happen to think you are hot, and my life has been kind of a mess for a while, so we can figure things out together. What do you say?"

"I say that's a good idea." I kissed him again. "What do you say we get out of here, go back to my place for a little while and talk?"

"Sounds like a good idea," he replied, lacing his fingers with mine as we headed back to the group to say our goodbyes. I didn't see Ethan, and that was fine with me. He could go off and do his detective thing and have a great life.

Joe and I were quiet on the way back to my place, and that was also fine. I was stuck in my head, replaying everything that Ethan had said to me. He had told me that I loved him, but he was wrong. I didn't love Ethan. I mean, I did love him, we were close, but I wasn't *in love* with him. How could I possibly be in love with Ethan? He was like a brother to me—except when we were sleeping together—then he wasn't.

I thought back to the other day and how he had mixed my coffee just how I like it; he'd even made the bed and rolled back the comforter two inches. He had ordered my breakfast, but if I'd called to order his, I wouldn't have known what to get him without asking him first. And the fruit cup! He'd made sure that there was no pineapple in it. Was there anything that he didn't like to eat?

"You alright?" Joe asked as we pulled into my townhouse development.

"Yeah, I was just thinking about what someone said tonight."

He chuckled. "He sure did say a lot."

I frowned as I looked at him. "Are you talking about Ethan? I wasn't thinking about him. He's not worth the time."

Joe didn't say anything else as we got out of his car and headed toward my door. After we were inside, I asked him if he wanted a glass of wine. He said yes as he shifted around my living room, looking over the pictures. I let my gaze slide over the many frames and frowned. Jesus, Ethan was in a lot of them.

"You guys *are* close to that family." He grinned over his shoulder at me.

"Oh, yes, we spent almost every holiday with them growing up. We still celebrate major events and birthdays with them."

"There are six of them and six of you?"

"Yeah, although we have four boys in our family, and they have four girls."

He laughed before he sipped from his wineglass after we were seated on the couch. "Almost perfect matches," he commented, and I frowned.

"What do you mean?"

"I mean, four boys and two girls, and four girls and two boys. Surprised you all never hooked up—but I guess a few of you did though, huh?" he asked, studying me carefully.

I sighed. "You want to talk about what Ethan said, don't you?"

He cocked a brow. "He did say quite a bit, Riley. I guess I don't want the details, but I would like to know if there is anything I should be concerned about."

I leaned back on the sofa. "Ethan and I had an arrangement. We didn't particularly date, but we did hook up. For lack of better words, he was kind of my best friend, and anytime I had too much to drink, he would take me home, which usually led to us in bed."

"How often did you two have sex?"

I tucked my bottom lip under my teeth as I thought about it. "I don't know. I guess it started about five or six years ago. We just hooked up one night, and we kept doing it every once in a while. Neither of us was ever in a relationship with someone else when we did. It was a thing of convenience." I shrugged.

"I have a feeling it might have been more casual for you than for him."

"What makes you say that?"

He stared at me. "Anyone can see that he's in love with you, Riley."

I tossed my head back and laughed. "Ethan doesn't love me. He tolerates me, Joe, and enjoys sex with me. That's it."

Joe smirked. "You don't see it." He took a swallow of his wine. "I think everyone at the party knows how he feels, except you. Everyone was very nice about it, which is the only reason I didn't feel uncomfortable, but it was obvious that they all knew it. I saw it when I went to get your beer."

"I think you are wrong."

"Well, as long as you don't feel the same way about him."

I stared him straight in the eye. "I am not in love with Ethan."

Joe remained quiet for a moment, then he took my wineglass from my hand and set both of our drinks on the coffee table. After that, he scooted closer to me and took my face in his hands and spoke huskily. "Then lucky me."

Joe kissed me, and I melted into him. Our kisses grew more in-depth, and before I realized what was happening, we were removing our clothing. Sadly, my mind was a million miles away and not in the moment. I was trying to find a way to stop our forward momentum, but the alcohol in my system made the sexual feelings too hard to deny.

Luckily, his cellphone rang, and he sighed as he removed his mouth from my breast. "That's Chip."

I nodded as he grabbed his phone off the coffee table and sat up. "Everything okay, Chip?"

He listened for a moment and frowned. "Okay, I'll be home soon. Let her know."

He hung up the phone and turned his sexy hazel eyes my way, letting them slide hungrily over my body. He put his palm on my stomach and slipped it up between my breasts. "As much as I hate to leave, I gotta go. Sasha had a nightmare."

"Absolutely," I said as I sat up and reached for my shirt. "Kids come first."

He cupped my cheek. "Thanks for understanding, Riley."

As we got dressed, my eyes landed on a picture of Henley, me, and Ethan. Suddenly, I needed Joe to leave as quickly as he could. Everywhere in my room, I saw Ethan, and I wasn't sure if I wanted to scream or cry.

I walked Joe to the door, kissed him good night, and told him that I had a good evening. I did like the man; he was excellent company, and for once, I could see myself going on more than three dates—maybe.

After I'd locked the door and turned off the lights, I'd grabbed the wine bottle off the counter and made a beeline for my bed. I was barely onto it before I started sobbing.

CHAPTER SIX

ETHAN

"What is your problem?" Cara asked me as I stared at the beer bottle in front of me. We had just finished our shifts, my last one at my local police station, and her as a pilot on our hospital medivac team. My sister had been a helicopter pilot in the Army, and when she decided to get out after ten years, she was lucky to get the job that she did.

Not only was she a pilot, but she was a paramedic too. She could pull double duty, behind the stick or on the patient. Out of all of us in the family, she was the one with the brains. She was also the one that pushed all of us to do our best while growing up.

"Nothing," I replied to her.

"Oh, cut the crap, Ethan. You've been moping around since the party. She doesn't love you. I know that hurts, but you need to let it go and move on. Obviously, Riley is not as worthy of you as we all thought."

"I appreciate you saying that, Cara, but she is to me—or she *was* to me. Not anymore, I guess. I'm glad I'm leaving town for a while. It will be good for me. I can focus on my career and forget about her." Forget about the fact that it has been precisely twenty days since I last held her in my arms.

"You'll never forget about her, little brother, but maybe you can put some distance between your heart and her."

I inhaled slowly and released it. "I know." I peered at Cara and smiled. "You know that is kind of the reason I decided to take the polygraph class. I'd never been interested in that kind of thing before, but what better way to put her behind me than twelve weeks away? Besides, it will give me a nice niche in the county."

"Very true, but just don't put the rest of us behind you once you become a big bad county detective." She pushed her shoulder against mine as she chuckled.

"No way! I could never do that."

"Well, you never know. You plan on moving closer to Stock Ridge?"

I took a drink of my beer. "Who knows. I want to get settled into my position first before I think about selling my place. I'm still in the county, so I'm okay for now."

"Yeah, but you're as far away from Stock Ridge as you can be. That will be a hell of a commute in the winter."

She held her bottle out to me, and I tapped mine to hers. "True."

"When do you leave for the class?"

"Sunday, June sixth. Class doesn't start until Monday morning, but I'm flying in the day before to get checked in and ready."

"Smart, are we going to do a big send-off?"

"No, I'd prefer a small dinner with the family. I don't need a party, and I don't want to travel on Sunday with a hangover." I laughed as I told her. A big part of it was that I didn't want another run-in with Riley.

"I think that is a good idea. You've grown up, Ethan Winston."

"You're like five years older than me, Cara. Sometimes you talk like you're my mother."

"God knows that I stressed enough over you when you were in high school, and I was overseas."

"You miss it?"

"Eh, sometimes. I miss the adrenaline rushes from the intense training and the missions we went on. I don't miss being shot at or some of the things that I saw."

"Yeah, I hear that."

"You will have your own war stories soon." She grinned my way.

"Oh, I already have enough of those from ten years in law enforcement."

"Yeah, but if you think the weirdos around here are bad, just wait until you get to see what the sickos in the rest of the county are like."

I laughed. "That is true."

MEMORIAL DAY CAME AND WENT, and I was glad that Riley didn't attend the picnic that we had. I hadn't seen her since Coral's party three weeks earlier, and I wasn't in a hurry to do so. There were times when I regretted what I'd said to her and the way I had walked off with her date staring at us. It wasn't classy; that's for sure.

My new job was going great, although I hadn't done much more than keep my eyes open, attend briefings, watch interviews, and tag along behind the other guys. I had a lot to learn, and I was willing to do everything that I could.

Dinner with the family on Saturday night before I left for training was excellent. Well, it was more than excellent. It was only the eight of us, like old times, and we laughed and joked like we always had growing up. It was hard to believe that all of us were in our thirties now, and we all had stable careers, and ironically, all single for the most part. I knew Coral was dating, but as of now, it was nothing serious. Evan had just split from his long-time girlfriend of four years when she decided to take a new job out west. Cara had previously been engaged but called it off for some odd reason, and Candy was married for less than a year before she filed for divorce with irreconcilable differences. I still have no idea what those differences were, but I respected her privacy. Neither Cara nor Candy seemed interested in dating now, and both threw themselves into their work. I guess it was my turn to do that, too, because we already knew how messed up my love life was.

I hugged all my siblings as they left, spent a few minutes with my parents, and then headed home to make sure I had all my stuff packed. I was just kicking back on the couch with a beer when there was a knock on the door. Probably Evan coming to hang out one last time.

When I pulled the door open, I froze for a second. "What are you doing here, Riley?"

"You're leaving tomorrow, right?"

"Yes."

"Can we talk?"

Riley looked unusually nervous as she asked, and that's what made me step back and let her in. It had nothing to do with the fact that I hadn't seen her in four weeks or that my heart started racing at the sight of her. "Do you want a beer?"

She shook her head. "No, I'll only take a moment of your time."

"Okay, what did you want to say?" I positioned myself on the other side of the kitchen island, setting my beer down and placing my palms flat on the cold surface. I had to keep my distance. One more night, and I was gone for twelve weeks.

"I wanted to apologize, Ethan. I acted horrible, and I know I did."

"Alright." I wanted to ask her which time she was apologizing for, the morning I dropped her off at her truck or the night at the party. I didn't, though. I just waited.

"That's all you're going to say?"

I shrugged. "What do you want me to say, Riley? You made it extremely clear that my feelings for you were not reciprocated. You also told me to butt out of your life. I have officially butted out."

"Yeah, by running away."

I stared at her. "Running away? Riley, I took another job. I'm not running away."

"But what about this training? It's three months long, Ethan. You can't say that you would have gone if things were different between us."

I jerked back. What the hell was she doing? "Riley, what are you saying? Are you trying to tell me that you love me?"

She shook her head. "No, I'm not saying that. I'm just saying that if I told you that, you wouldn't be running off to some stupid training in Georgia of all places. You had an excellent job here in Millerstown. Why did you have to move up to the county?"

"Why? Maybe because I want more. Maybe because I want to be a detective and not a beat cop my whole life."

"Being a beat cop was always enough before. Why has it changed?"

"What's the big deal to you, which position I hold? You worried that I won't be around to pick you up after a night out with your friends? Or keep your bed warm? Did you already break up with the Newman guy?"

She pursed her lips. "That is not it! Jesus, Ethan, we are friends. Best friends! We have been that way since high school. I talk to you about everything, and yeah, so we sleep together, but it's not like you don't enjoy it."

She had come around the kitchen island, and I shook my

head. "That's not the point, Ry," I told her as I turned to face her. "And you're right, we *were* best friends, Riley, but I need more. I want more, not just from you, but from my career. I have wanted to be a detective since I graduated from the police academy; you *know* that. I finally got what I have been working toward. You should wish me good luck, not whine about how I am leaving you."

"But you are leaving me, Ethan!"

I snapped as I took a step forward. "You need to grow up, Riley. You are thirty-two years old! I am not a fucking toy that someone is taking away from you." I grabbed her face. "I'm a man who is in love with you, and no matter what I do, what I say, what I show you—you just don't see that! I can't sit around here any longer waiting to see if you will ever love me!"

Tears began to fill her eyes, and for Riley to cry, that was harsh. She never cried. She grabbed my arms. "Please don't go, Ethan. Don't leave me. I know I'm selfish, but I need you right now."

A tear slipped down her cheek, and I couldn't help myself; I crushed her mouth to mine, and she clung to me. I kissed her harder than I ever had, showing her every ounce of my passion and love for her, and then I leaned our foreheads together.

"As much as I love you, Riley. As much as I want you to love me, I know you never will." I cupped her cheeks, breathing her in for a moment. "I have to move on with my life. That kiss was my goodbye to you." I stepped back, dropping my arms. "I can't wait any longer. I deserve more. I deserve to be loved back."

"I do love you," she said as another tear raced down her cheek.

"Yeah, like a brother, not like a man. It's not enough." She glanced away and swallowed, and I held my hand up. "Don't bother trying to come up with something, Riley. It's over. I should have stopped this a long time ago. I hope you find what you want. I just hope you can be happy for me someday."

I started to step around her, but she jumped in front of me and put her hands on my chest. "Ethan, we can't end things this way. Please!"

"Riley, what do you want me to do? Come on! I'm trying to let you go. Why do you have to make this so fucking difficult!"

"I'm—" She started to say something, then closed her mouth and looked away. I watched her wilt right in front of me. Her shoulders rolled forward as shadows crossed her features. It was something I had never seen her do before, and it almost broke my heart. "I'm sorry," her voice was soft. "I'll go. I'm so sorry I interrupted your night."

She turned and walked away, and I had to force myself not to follow her. My chest hurt, my gut felt sick, and my mind was in an uproar.

At the door, she paused but didn't look back. "I do wish you the best, Ethan. Take care of yourself."

She opened the door and slipped out into the night, and I could hear her crying as she ran down my front stairs to my driveway. I rushed to the door, my hand on the knob to turn it, but something stopped me.

My future was someplace else. I would get over Riley, and she would learn to live without me. We'd be fine. I put my forehead against the door, listening to her car start and back out of the driveway. It wasn't until after her car pulled away that I opened the door and stared out into the dark and quiet night.

I wondered for a moment if I should have gone after her. I shook my head and sighed as I closed the door, turned the lock, and shut off the lights before going to my room.

In bed, I lay there and thought back over a lot of my life. I remembered good times and bad—many with Riley—several without—and I laughed a little and shed a few tears, then I rolled over and closed my eyes. Tomorrow a new day would begin and with it a new journey.

CHAPTER SEVEN

RILEY

I hadn't seen Ethan face-to-face since the night of Coral's birthday. That didn't mean I hadn't seen him. I had. Every freaking time I looked around my home, I saw him. He was in almost every single picture scattered over every surface. He had helped me pick out the sofa. He'd fixed my washer. He'd hung the photos in the living room; he'd even gone to the freaking grocery store for me!

There wasn't a place in my house that didn't have memories attached that included him. Even my freaking toilet, as he'd many times held my hair back as I'd gotten sick. It was driving me nuts. I was ready to sell my townhouse and find a new place to live that had no memories of him.

I had just gotten home from work, and I was staring into my fridge. I was hungry, but then again, I wasn't. I wanted to eat, but my stomach had been iffy whenever I put something into it over the last couple of days. I was probably coming down with one of the stomach bugs that got passed around so quickly in school.

I sighed as I closed the fridge door when the doorbell rang. I glanced at the clock. It was only four-thirty, too early for my date with Joe. He wasn't supposed to be here until five, and then we were taking the kids to the movies and out to dinner.

Our relationship over the last few weeks was progressing—slowly. I really did enjoy spending time with Joe, and last week, he'd told the kids that we were good friends hanging out. Chip didn't seem to care one way or the other, but Sasha was excited that her older brother's teacher was friends with her father.

Because he had such a busy schedule with his job and the kids, I didn't get to see him too often, which was a plus. I couldn't get tired of him, and I appreciated how important his kids were to him. I did love the fact that they always came first.

I pulled open the door to see Henley. "What are you doing here?"

I left the door open and went back into the kitchen. If we weren't eating until after the movie, I had to have something other than popcorn or candy. However, the theater did have soft pretzels with lots of gooey cheese. That sounded awesome.

"He leaves Sunday," he said as he closed the door behind him.

"Who?" I asked casually as if I had no clue who he was referring to. Of course, I knew that Ethan left on Sunday. Everyone in our family and a few of his siblings had all made sure to remind me.

"You know damn well who, Ry. You need to go talk to him."

"No, I don't. If Ethan wants to apologize to me for what he said, then he can come to find me. Until then, I have nothing to say to him."

"Jesus, you are as hardheaded as a brick." He leaned against the counter and crossed his arms.

"I am not the hardheaded one. Talk to him. Besides, you should be pissed off at him for calling me a drunk."

"You are," he snapped back.

My face turned to him so quickly that it almost kept going all the way around. "What?"

"Riley, everyone knows you drink too much. Ethan's right. You have a problem."

"I do not!" I yanked open the fridge, my eyes falling on the wine bottle in there, and I almost yanked it out. Instead, I dug around in the drawer and pulled out my lunch meat. "I can't believe all of you think I have a damn drinking problem. I can drink or not drink. It's my choice." Damn, I wanted a drink right then.

"You should choose not to drink," he stated, and I rolled my eyes at him.

I pulled open the bag of ham and began to reach in, but the smell of the ham wafted up to my nose, and my stomach rolled over on itself. I tossed the ham to the side and leaned over the sink as my stomach heaved.

"Shit." Henley was at my side, pulling my hair back and turning the water on to wash down my vomit. "How long have you been sick?" His hand slipped over my brow, and I pushed it away.

"I guess I picked something up at school, or that lunch meat is bad."

Henley picked up the bag, sniffing the contents. "Smells fine." He pulled a piece out and stuffed it in his mouth. "Tastes fine, too. Anything else bothering you?"

"No. I just need some ginger ale and to sit down for a few minutes."

"Okay, go sit. I'll get your drink."

I plopped on the couch, and the nausea in my stomach started to recede. I should call Joe and let him know I needed to cancel, but my phone was in the kitchen and getting up was too much of a hassle. Instead, I leaned my head back until Henley brought me the glass.

He waited until I'd taken a few sips and then sighed as he sat down. "Riley, I don't want to argue with you or upset you, but Ethan's not the only one that sees it."

"See's what?" I asked him, totally at a loss.

"What you are doing to yourself. You drink way too much."

"Are you serious? You're going to get on me again about that?"

He put his hand on my arm. "Look, you're my little sister. I love you to death, but I am worried about you. Ethan is too. You need to go see him and say goodbye before he leaves."

"Why? He didn't even bother to tell me that he was leaving."

"He told you when he told everyone else."

"He should have told me sooner. I'm his best friend."

"*No*, I'm his best friend. You're the woman he loves."

I closed my eyes and groaned. "Ethan does not love me, Hen."

"He does, Ry. How can you not see it?"

I burst off the couch. "Maybe I don't want to see it. Or maybe it doesn't matter to me how he feels about me." I walked away to get my phone.

Henley laughed. "If it didn't matter to you what he felt, then you wouldn't be so bent out of shape. Riley, all of us have been waiting for you to wake up and realize how much you care about him. There is not one person in either of our families that doesn't think you two shouldn't be together. You are the only one."

"Why does everyone think we need to be together? Everyone needs to just get it through their stupid head that I am not in love with Ethan, and I never will be."

He shook his head as he stared at the floor. "Fine, I give up. Have it your way. Be miserable. Whatever." He tossed his hands into the air.

I watched him leave and then frowned at the closed door. I grabbed my phone to tell Joe I wasn't feeling well, but I realized that I felt better. Maybe it was all in my head.

❄

OR MAYBE IT wasn't all in my head. After the movie, we went to get pizza, and the minute I tried to bite into my slice, I dropped my food to the plate and excused myself. I rushed to the bathroom where I barely made it to the commode before I barfed again.

I was running cold water over my wrists when Sandra, our waitress, stepped into the bathroom. "You okay? You looked a little green out there."

"I guess I have picked up a stomach bug." I laughed.

"Oh, those are going around. I thought maybe you were pregnant. I saw the way you reacted to the food. I was like that when I was pregnant with both my boys. Could barely eat at all the first trimester."

I forced out a laugh as my mind suddenly went into overdrive. Pregnant? No, no, no, no, no!

Sandra went into one of the stalls, and I touched my breast. It was tender. Hadn't I wondered why my breasts were so sore just yesterday?

The world started to spin around me, and I clung to the sink for a moment. There was no way. I was on the pill! I pulled my shoulders back and stared at my reflection—it wasn't possible. Oh my god, it couldn't be possible. I shook my hair back and left the bathroom to return to the table.

I nibbled on my piece of pizza but found that it caused my stomach to roll, so I ate a breadstick instead. As the kids ate, they talked nonstop about the movie, and Joe listened to their every word.

He was a good father. My hand landed against my lower belly. Was I pregnant? Was it possible? Oh crap! I was trying not to panic as I started counting back in my head to my last period. My periods were always light, and I never paid much attention to them.

Joe put his hand on my knee under the table, and I smiled at him. "You okay?" He asked. "You didn't eat much."

"Yeah, I guess I filled up on pretzels." I laughed to make light of it.

After dinner, Joe dropped me off and walked me to the door. "You sure you are okay? You were awful quiet tonight."

"I'm not feeling all that hot. I think I might be coming down with something."

He cupped my cheek and kissed my brow. "Well, then I hope you feel better. Get some rest, and I'll talk to you later."

I let myself into my house and went straight to the calendar where I kept track of my monthly cycle. I flipped back another page. Holy crap! I had missed my period!

I grabbed my purse and my car keys and rushed out to my car. Instead of going to our local pharmacy, I drove two towns over. Everyone in Millerstown knew my family or me, and god forbid someone saw me buy a pregnancy test! It would be all over town before I could even take it!

I was home forty minutes later, staring at the back of the stick, praying that this was a waste of money. I peed on it and let it sit on the counter. The whole time, I told myself that I had just wasted an hour. It was going to be negative, and I was getting sick instead.

When the time was up, I lifted the stick, said a small prayer, and turned it over. I stared at it, my knees going weak as I slithered to the floor in front of my sink. Oh, my god! I was pregnant. I put my head back against the cabinet and closed my eyes. What in the hell was I going to do?

I thought back to dinner and how I thought Joe was such an amazing father. Sadly, I knew without a doubt that this child wasn't his.

I dropped the stick and put my face to my hands. There was no way I could tell Ethan. Wait, if I told him, would he stay here?

It didn't matter if he left or stayed. I needed to tell him. I just didn't know if I could.

✳

SATURDAY NIGHT, I knew that he was having dinner with his family. Coral had mentioned it when I stopped to get coffee this morning. I told her that I wanted to surprise him with a going away gift and asked her to let me know when he had gone home after dinner.

My hands started shaking the minute that I had received the text from her, and as I stood outside his door, I could barely control the quiver in them. What was he going to say?

It turns out that he had a lot to say, but not about the pregnancy. I couldn't even get those words out of my mouth. Not with how angry he was. It was all I could do to get out of there before I broke down. The minute the door closed, I started to sob and ran to my car. I pulled out of his driveaway and drove away as quickly as I could. When I was far enough away that I knew he wouldn't see me, I pulled over and bawled like a baby.

I wasn't sure what I was crying for, but I knew that I had messed things up badly, and I wasn't sure how to fix them.

CHAPTER EIGHT

ETHAN

*L*eaving town was kind of tough, especially after the way things ended last night with Riley. I'd thought about stopping by her place a least a dozen times, but I had a plane to catch, and Evan was dropping me off at the airport.

Riley didn't love me, didn't want me, so why should I stick around and put myself through it all? I shouldn't.

I had a future in front of me. A new career path that needed my attention, and I was determined to put my all into it. It was going to be rough, but I would get over her—eventually.

Evan and I chatted on the way to the airport, and then he wished me well and left me standing at the terminal to start my adventure. By mid-afternoon, I was in my rental car and heading to the training center where I'd be staying for the next twelve weeks.

The training center was huge and did a lot more than just polygraph. There were all kinds of law enforcement courses there, including tactical and forensic. Because they had so many classes, they had dorms. There was a specific dorm for the people in my class, call the Liar's Den. I chuckled as I pulled open the door. There were twenty people in the class, and we would all be in this one building. We had private rooms, although I found that we shared a bathroom with three other people in our quad. We had a good-sized common area with a huge television, pool table, dartboard, and a large kitchen with several tables to accommodate all of us.

There were already two guys there when I arrived, both at least ten years older than me and evidently very seasoned detectives. Man, I was going to have a lot to learn and prove here. I wondered as I got myself unpacked if I would be the youngest guy here.

I checked emails, answered a few texts, and then went to find dinner. In the tavern right down the street, two women were laughing loudly in the corner. One had long honey-blond hair very similar to Riley's, and I suddenly wished that I could change tables. I didn't want to do that, but I did switch seats so that my back was to her.

I made it through dinner and returned to my room, pulling out my laptop to read over some information about the class starting tomorrow. When I finished, I put a movie on my computer and started to watch it. I almost went out to the common room, but I heard laughter, and I recognized it as the women from the tavern. Nope. I sure as hell was not ready for that.

The next day, I was up early and started my day with a run. I took off and found a local park with a trail near a small creek. I was walking a circle in the parking lot to cool down when the two women from last night jogged up and stopped.

"Whew! That last half mile was rough!" the blonde said.

I chuckled, forcing myself to be friendly and not turn my back on her. She looked way too much like Riley, for my liking. "How far did you run?"

"Oh, it was supposed to be six miles, but we only managed four," the brunette said.

The blonde added, "We realized that we shouldn't have had that last beer last night." She grinned as she tried to calm her breathing, pacing back and forth in front of me. Her hair was almost exactly the same color as Riley's. I looked away from her and studied the brunette. She was very athletic-looking, and while she seemed slightly winded, she wasn't huffing as bad as her friend.

"Are you here for the polygraph class?" the blonde asked.

"Yeah, I assume you guys are too?" I wasn't going to say that I had heard them last night.

"Yep, we're from upstate New York," the blonde replied. She turned to her friend. "I still can't believe we were lucky enough to be sent together."

The brunette smiled at her friend and then stepped forward, holding out her hand. "Samantha Revels, and this is Vera Williams."

I shook her hand. "Ethan Winston, I'm from central PA." Vera shook my hand after I let go of Samantha's.

"How old are you?" Vera asked as she studied me carefully.

"Um, thirty-two, why?"

"Glad to see we aren't the only young ones here. How long have you been a detective?"

I grinned at them. "Would you believe less than two weeks?"

Vera laughed. "You're kidding."

I shook my head. "Nope. I've been on the force for ten years but worked for a small municipal department. I just got hired at the county level, and the guy who was supposed to come couldn't make it, so my first assignment was here."

"Wow! That's a hell of a training for your first month in investigations," Samantha remarked.

"You're telling me. Well, I guess I'll see you guys in class. I'm going to head in and shower before I find breakfast."

I couldn't get away from them fast enough. Vera was just a little bit too much like Riley, and it put me on edge. How was I going to get over the woman if I had a freaking look-alike in my class for the next three months?

I HAD plenty of time to shower, dress, and grab the breakfast that I found was being provided for us today. Usually, we'd have to get our own, but they were kind enough to supply it today, knowing that many of us wouldn't know where the stores were yet.

I collected my stuff, refilled my travel coffee mug, and made my way to the classroom. It was a large room with oversized comfy office chairs and charging stations for our computers. As we checked in, we were told that we'd already been partnered and were given assigned seats to make it easier for all the instructors to get to know us. On the front of our desks were engraved nameplates that included our departments and states. Well, that was nice.

I grinned to myself as I read Detective Ethan Winston in front of my seat. I was only seated for about two minutes before a hand landed on my shoulder and a soft voice whispered into my ear, "Aw, too bad we aren't partners."

I shifted to look up at Vera. "Oh, yeah, that's too bad," I commented, but damn if I wasn't glad that we weren't. It was bad enough that she was sitting right behind me in the class-room, and I was so pleased when a man a few years older than me took the seat to my right.

"Tim Sanders," he introduced himself before he took a seat. As others came in, we struck up a casual conversation that Vera tried to jump into several times. Finally, Tim turned her way and gave her the attention she'd been looking for, and I logged into the Wi-Fi and checked my new department email.

Holy shit, I had checked it an hour ago, but I already had fifteen more emails since then. I skimmed over them as the rest of the people got situated and then happily sat back as three instructors got us started.

They introduced themselves and gave a little biography before they started offering a rundown of what we would be learning over the next twelve weeks. Our classes would run five days a week for eight hours. We'd get an hour for lunch and have at least three hours of homework every night. Week three and week eight, we had classes on Saturday. That way, on week five, we could have a four day weekend for Independence Day. If I went home, that cost was on me. I'd have to decide when we got closer.

The first part of the morning was all about the courses we would be taking and what they would expect of us. They talked about how those with lots of experience, like Walt Hammering, who had been a detective for fifteen years, would work with those who had less experience, and joy—they tossed my name out as the rookie detective in the room.

There were a few jokes about my badge being so shiny new that it was going to blind them all, and how my partner needed a towel to wipe the wetness from behind my ears, but it was all in good fun.

At ten, we had a break, and by eleven we had started our first class. I knew by lunch that I was going to love and hate the next twelve weeks. There were going to be some incredibly hard things to learn and scenarios that were going to test me in ways that I'd never imagined, but I was determined to do well.

We got out a little early that afternoon, and a few of us were talking about what we would do for dinner. A couple of the guys said they were hitting the diner or tavern a few miles away, but a few others spoke about finding the store and picking up meals that we might want to share.

Tim slapped me on the back, laughing. "I'll put money in for food, but I can't cook worth shit! If it's my night to cook, you all might want to think takeout."

Samantha joined our conversation, and we all decided that two of us would cook each night. Two different meals so people could choose what they wanted to eat. We set up a schedule, and those of us who were interested began to sign up for the first four weeks. With twenty of us in class, we would each cook two nights—or order takeout—and then clean two nights.

We made a sign-up, and I ended up taking the first shift. "Might as well get it over with," I said as I stepped back. Samantha sidled up next to me. "What are you making?"

I inhaled and thought about it for a moment. "Probably pasta." I laughed. "That's pretty easy and quick for a group like this."

"Anyone not like pasta?" she asked, and no one said they didn't. She turned to me. "I'll help you make a huge batch and a big salad. What do you think?"

"Works for me," I told her, and she put her name down next to mine.

Four of us decided to head to the store together to pick up food for tonight and tomorrow, and after dropping our stuff off in our rooms, I met them in the parking lot. We climbed into one of the guys' personal SUVs and quickly fell into conversation. By the time we got back from the store, I knew that I had several new friends that I would never forget, one of them being Sam.

I didn't want to be interested in her, but she intrigued me. She was a few years older than me, divorced with a preteen, and she was funny. She was comfortable in her skin and made as much fun of herself as she did others.

We unloaded the food, and Samantha and I claimed the kitchen and kicked everyone else out. Vera tried to join us, but Samantha shoed her away, saying too many cooks in the kitchen. Vera didn't seem happy about that, and I wondered if her pout was as practiced as Riley's usually was.

By the time dinner was over, I was ready to kick back, get

my homework done, and get some rest. It wasn't until I was lying on my bed that I pulled my phone out and read through all the messages I had from this afternoon.

I'd seen them come through, but I'd forced myself to keep my attention on what I was doing. Several guys wished me luck. Cara was checking to see how it was going, and Henley asked if I missed home yet. I sighed when I saw there was no message from Riley.

Not that I expected there to be, but maybe part of me was hoping that she would have sent me something like maybe I'm sorry, or I miss you.

I set my phone off to the side and pulled out my book to start working on my homework. I had come here to forget about her, and that's what I needed to do.

CHAPTER NINE

RILEY

The week after Ethan left was long and stressful. I spent most of my time when I wasn't working, alone and at home. I went by my parents in the morning and took care of Buttercup and Fellow, and then I'd head back home before either of my parents were up.

Mom had called me mid-week and asked if I was sleeping alright since I was there so early, but I told her I had a busy schedule this week and needed to adjust my hours a bit. She seemed to buy it and let it go.

I was having significant issues eating anything that contained meat. The moment I smelled it, I would get sick. My lunches revolved around tomato soup, cheese sandwiches, and bland salads. By dinnertime, I could eat a little bit of meat, but I couldn't cook it. I got takeout a few times that week instead.

Several times I looked at my GYN's phone number and considered calling them, but I wasn't sure what I was going to do yet. I was only five weeks pregnant, so I had time to decide. I'd even looked up a clinic address in the next county over and read over their webpage.

When I was home, I researched adoption, abortion, and

carrying a baby to term repeatedly. Maybe I was hoping that I'd receive a sign about what I should do.

I didn't want an abortion. I didn't personally have an issue with someone if that was their choice, but I didn't want it to be mine. I knew that plenty of families out there would be thrilled to have a baby if I decided to give it up for adoption.

But if I put the child up for adoption, would I tell Ethan? Didn't I have to tell him? I think that by law, I did, but if I went away for several months, took a leave of absence, no one would ever know—right?

I rubbed my hands over my face. I would know.

If I told Ethan, I was pretty sure that he would refuse to put the child up for adoption. Then he'd probably take the child for himself, and how the hell could I live around here and watch my child grow up with him and not be part of its life?

I had concluded that the only two choices I had were to abort the child, and no one would ever know, or have the baby and tell Ethan about it. I could assure him that he didn't need to be part of the child's life. Hell, if he said that he didn't want anything to do with the baby, then I could put the baby up for adoption.

I wiped tears from my face. I hadn't cried this much since I was a teenager and Billy Wolfe had broken my heart by ditching me at prom and leaving with my best friend.

I closed the browser on my computer and stared at the picture on my desktop. It was of Ethan and me, and I touched his face on the screen. I missed him—missed him so damn much that it physically hurt. Whenever I thought of him, my chest ached.

I curled up on the bed and stared at my phone, bringing up his contact information and then reading over our previous text message conversations. I laughed a few times at his wise-ass comments, let a few tears fall, and wished that I dared to call him.

I couldn't, though, because this wasn't a conversation that I could have with him over the phone. I would have to wait for Ethan to come back. Then I would sit down and tell him what was going on. I knew from Henley that he was probably going to be home for the Fourth of July weekend.

That meant that I had almost three weeks to make a decision and come up with the words to tell him if need be.

ETHAN HAD BEEN GONE three weeks now, and I knew that in another week, he would be home for a visit. At least that was the plan so far from Henley. I had yet to make my decision, but I wasn't hiding at home anymore.

Even though I didn't know what I was going to do, I had decided that I should at least see my doctor, get it confirmed, and speak to them a little bit about my options. Maybe they would tell me what I should do.

By my calculations, I was almost eight weeks pregnant, and while no one else could tell, I was starting to see the changes in my body. Just this morning, I'd noticed the swelling in my lower belly. I knew the baby was still this tiny thing and mostly a head, as the brain began to develop, but my body was preparing itself to go the long haul. Was I mentally ready to go with it?

I was sitting in front of the medical building, having arrived a few minutes early and not ready to face reality quite yet. A door opened off to the side, and two people stepped out. I started to smile when I saw it was Richard and Rebecca Winston, but then I noticed their faces.

They both looked stricken as if they had just received the worst news they ever could have heard. Richard had his arm around Rebecca and supported her as they walked slowly toward the parking lot. My eyes followed them to the car, and I could see the anguish in their features.

My jaw hung open as I watched him help her into the car, and then he closed the door and stepped toward the back of it, putting his hand on the roof to steady himself before he wiped a hand over his face. He rounded the car and put on a brave face before opening the driver's door and getting in. I saw them speak for a moment, and then he lifted his face toward mine, looked away immediately, and left.

I turned to see where they had come from and read the words on the door. It was an oncologist. Tears sprang forward as my hand went to my mouth. One of them had cancer, and it was a horrible diagnosis. Remembering the look on Rebecca's face, I had a feeling it was her.

My hand flitted to my belly, and I pressed lightly. Did any of the kids know? Did Ethan know? Suddenly I pictured the little being in my stomach, and I stood and walked into my doctor's office. My decision was made.

ON TUESDAY, I found an excuse to stop over and see Rebecca. I brought her some of her favorite jam that I had intentionally picked up. We sat at the kitchen table, spooning some of the sweet jam onto crackers while we sipped tea. We talked for a while, and I asked her questions about growing up.

When I went to leave, I found Richard on the back porch. "Mighty nice of you to visit with Rebecca."

I smiled at him. "It was my pleasure. I always love hearing her stories."

"Is there any specific reason you wanted to hear them now?" he asked as he continued to rock and stare out over the backyard.

I nibbled my bottom lip as I approached him and sighed. "I saw you coming out of the doctors the other day."

He nodded. "I thought that was you." He turned and looked at me. "You haven't said anything to anyone?"

I shook my head as I took a seat beside him. "No, I didn't. How bad is it, Richard?"

He glanced at me, and blinked a few times. "As bad as it can be, I'm afraid."

"Richard, I'm so sorry." I reached for his hand and squeezed it. "When are you going to tell everyone?"

"We want to wait until Ethan comes home. We decided it would be easier to do it all at once, and I don't want to tell him while he's trying to focus on his class." He turned to look at me. "You won't say anything, will you?"

"Absolutely not! Although I think I should say something to my mother. I think it would be good for her to know. She can help with whatever you need."

"Maybe you might mention it to her. I'm not sure I could tell her, not right now."

"I will do that. In fact, I will go over there right now and speak to my parents, and I'll make sure that they know not to tell anyone else." I paused. "Richard, did the doctor suggest any treatment?"

He shook his head sadly. "There is no treatment."

My heart ached at his words. "Was he able to say how long she might have?"

He lifted his chin, blinking a few times, and I saw the tears shimmer in his eyes. "Days, maybe a few weeks at most. They want to put her on hospice immediately."

Tears ran silently down my cheeks. I could not imagine the pain and fear he was feeling. I squeezed his hand again. "I love you guys. Please let me know if there is anything that I can do. I'll come to visit her again tomorrow."

"She would like that, Riley. Thank you, sweetheart."

I kissed his cheek and made it inside my car before I put my head back against the seat and sobbed. Oh, Ethan! I cannot imagine what you are about to go through.

THE CONVERSATION with my parents was hard, and my mother was devastated. They both promised to keep it quiet until Ethan returned, and everyone could learn at once. She told me that she'd check in with them the next morning and see to anything they might need. I told her I'd check in the afternoons.

That's what we did for the next two days. I stopped in the afternoon and cooked for them. Then I'd sit with Rebecca and listen to her tell stories of her life if she wasn't too tired.

I asked if the other kids had been around, but she said that they were all busy. She knew that once they found out, they wouldn't leave her alone, and she hated the fact that it was going to disturb their busy lives.

"Oh, Rebecca, I don't even know what to say to you about that."

She took my hand. "You promise that you'll put aside whatever problem that you have with Ethan and be there for him after I go."

I held her hand tightly, swallowing the lump in my throat. "You know that I will."

She smiled at me softly. "He's going to make a good father."

I shifted back, my eyes going wide. Was she talking in generalities?

She patted my hand. "Riley, I was pregnant six times. I know what a pregnant woman looks like. I recognize the protective hand over the belly and the queasy stomach. Why do you think I made us ginger tea the other day? Both of us were feeling a bit under the weather. I assume you haven't told him yet." She paused. "It is his, isn't it?"

I closed my eyes briefly, sagging in my seat. "Yes, it is." That was the first time I had admitted it out loud to anyone. "And no one knows. Only my doctor."

She smiled sweetly. "How far along are you?"

"Eight weeks."

"And are you taking care of yourself?"

"I am. I had a doctor's appointment the day I saw you and Richard at the medical complex." I gnawed on my bottom lip for a moment. "Seeing you is what helped me make the decision."

"What decision?"

"To keep the baby. When I saw you, I knew something bad was happening, and there was no way that I could do anything bad to Ethan's child."

Rebecca studied me with light-blue eyes. "Riley, do you love my son?"

"I do, Rebecca."

"I mean, like a woman loves a man, not like a family member."

I tried to smile as I glanced around. "I want to think I do, but I'm not sure. I don't think I have ever been in love before, and I don't know how I feel about anything right now."

"Well, I think one day, you will know for sure. I personally think you do, but I know you need to figure that out on your own. I know that Ethan loves you more than life and would do anything for you, and he will be that way for his child. Please make sure that whatever you decide, you include him in the decisions of raising his child. Will you promise me that?"

"I promise, Rebecca." I held her hand as we both let tears drift down our cheeks. "I promise."

CHAPTER TEN

ETHAN

*C*lass was going smoothly, and we were moving right along. Our first section had only been one day. History and Evolution of Psychophysiological Detection of Deception, better known as Polygraph, introduced the whole process and how it started.

The next subject was the Mechanics of Instrument Operation. We discussed how to check the equipment's functionality and place the equipment properly on the test subject. Not only did we learn proper placement, but we were taught alternative placements for times that might be needed—say a person was missing an arm. That had taken two days to go through.

The third section was a little more intense as we started the Test Question Construction phase. We had to do a lot of thinking in that one, coming up with our own cases, test questions, and then do mock simulations in front of the class where the instructors helped us tweak our questions. I felt slightly out of my league during that section. There were a lot of people here with much more experience than me, and it showed here, but they were all helpful.

I learned early that a few people might laugh. Hell, the entire class might bust a gut, but they always helped come up with answers and ideas. I appreciated that more than I could have expressed.

We spent an entire week on Polygraph Techniques and several days on Pre-Test Interviews and Post Interviews. Next week it was all about Test Data Analysis, and then we'd have four days off for the Fourth of July holiday.

The days were the same, wake up and try not to think of Riley, work out and try not to think about her. Go to class and focus on my future, then have lunch with a few of the guys or ladies. I'd gotten used to Vera, although I still kept my distance. And lucky for me, I was able to keep Riley mostly at bay during the day.

After class, I'd work out, do homework, sometimes hang out with a few people, or help in the kitchen—even when it wasn't my turn. I always did enjoy cooking. After, I'd watch a movie, play cards or darts in the common room, or head back to my room and study more. Through the afternoon and evenings, I'd have to remind myself not to think of Riley continually. It was hard when the guys kept bringing up their wives or girlfriends.

At the end of my third week in class, I responded to a text from Henley, but instead of answering me via text, he called.

"Hey, buddy, what's going on? You got that lying test all figured out yet?"

I snickered. "I'm working on it. Hardest damn class I have ever attended. You know I've never been a brainy kind of guy. I hated college, squeaked by."

Henley laughed. "You are learning that you are smarter than you think. What else are you doing around there?"

"Not too much. Working out, taking class, studying, hanging out with the other people in my class—cooking a lot."

"Any hot women?"

I didn't even think as I responded. "Would you believe there is a woman here that looks a lot like Riley?" Henley was quiet, and I winced. "I keep my distance."

"I was gonna say."

"Actually, I have been hanging out with this one woman, Sam. She's from New York."

"Ah, okay. So, since you brought her up—have you tried to reach out to Riley at all?"

"I have nothing to say to your sister, and you know that, Lee."

He sighed. "Yeah, I know, but she hasn't been herself since you left. Like she's a different woman. She hasn't even gone out to the tavern since you left."

I stared at the ceiling. I didn't want to talk about Riley. When I thought about her, I thought about how much not only my heart but my dick missed her.

"I'm sure she's just wallowing in her own self-pity," I replied.

"No, I don't think that's it, Ethan. I think it has something to do with what you said the night before you left. What did you say to her?"

"I said a lot of things."

"Yeah, like what?" I ground my teeth, and he kept going. "Look, you might want to forget all about her and move on with your life, but I'm still here looking out for my sister. Something is wrong with her, and I'm trying to figure out what the hell it is. So tell me what the fuck you said to her before you left."

"I told her how I felt, but I told her I wasn't sticking around. I couldn't wait for her to come around. I can't keep doing that, Lee. You know it, and I know it. I was only enabling her erratic behavior. Maybe she is taking what I said seriously. Maybe she is growing up and realizing how damn selfish she has been."

"Or maybe she does love you, and you broke her fucking heart."

"Dude, I don't want to fight with you. You know how I feel about her or felt about her. This trip has done me good. I've focused on me, and I'm not thinking about her every damn minute of the day. I'm trying to move on with my life, and she needs to do that too."

There was a knock on my door, and I sat up and leaned forward to pull it open. Sam stood there, two beer bottles in her hand. I smiled at her as she leaned against the doorjamb. I lifted a finger to tell her to give me a minute.

"Look, I hope that she figures things out, but I'm not sure I can tell you anything that might help you. I gotta go; tell everyone I said hello, and I'll see you when I come home."

"Will you try to talk to her when you do?"

I frowned. "I don't know. I'm being honest here, Lee." I let my eyes drift up Sam's bare legs. She was wearing shorts and a t-shirt, and she looked pretty damn sexy in them. "I gotta move on with my life, man."

"What, with that woman you met there? Sam, was it?"

"Maybe," I commented, and my eyes latched on to hers. "I gotta go, Henley."

I hung up before I could hear what else he was going to say and stood, tossing my phone to the desk. "Is that beer for me?"

"Unless you want me to drink alone," she said and stepped into my room, holding the bottle out to me. I approached her, taking the bottle.

"I don't want to drink alone," I replied softly and reached past her to push the door closed.

"Neither do I," she commented and laid her other hand on my chest.

I set my beer off to the side and took hold of her face, pulling her lips to mine and kissing her slowly. When I pulled back, I stared down at her.

"Are you alright with this only being what it is here?" she asked.

"What do you mean?"

"I mean, no promises or commitments. I have a life in New

York. You have what sounds like a complicated one in Pennsylvania. How about we just enjoy what we have here, and when we leave, we kiss goodbye and go our separate ways."

I grinned. "As long as you are okay with that. I know I'm not in a place to give anyone anything else."

"Oh, yeah, I'm sure. It sounds like you have someone you are trying to get over, and well, I'm still kind of stuck on my ex-husband, so you don't have to worry about me getting all clingy. It's just sex."

"I can do just sex."

She leaned forward and nipped at my bottom lip. "Then let's do just sex, Detective Winston."

She didn't have to say another word as I wrapped my arms around her and blocked out Riley the best that I could. I reminded myself that she was seeing someone else, so she was probably having sex several times a week. There was nothing wrong with me having sex with Sam.

After we finished, I leaned back against my headboard and stared at the ceiling. Sam was curled against me, and then she sighed and sat up. "That was very nice."

I chuckled. "You know, if anyone else said that, I might get offended."

She grinned. "You can't say that it was earth-shattering for you either."

"No, I can't, but you are right. It was nice."

"Scratched the itch."

"It did."

She patted my chest. "Okay, then. I'm going to get dressed and get out of here."

"You do that." And she did. Over the weekend, we did that a couple more times, and Monday night, as we were lying in my bed, I contemplated something.

"Hey, you said you were staying here over break, right?"

"Yeah, Peter has Sadie at the beach for a few weeks."

"You're not going to go there?"

"Oh, god no! Peter's girlfriend is with them."

"Oh, yeah, that would suck." I hesitated. "You want to come back home with me?" Her eyes went wide, and I put my hand up. "No, not like that. Not as my girlfriend or with any strings. The offer is to get you out of here for a few days. You could check out how us country folks do police work in a small town."

She laughed. "You sure your family wouldn't mind?"

"Not at all. They are always welcoming of friends."

"They wouldn't think it was weird that you are bringing me back when we aren't an item?"

I shrugged. "We don't have to tell them that."

"What are you talking about, Ethan?" She laughed loudly, then she smirked. "Ah—you want it to look like you have moved on from Riley, don't you?"

I shook my head, but I was laughing. "No, okay, fine. Yeah, I guess that's stupid."

She squeezed my arm. "It's not stupid. I get it. I did the same thing with Peter. I dated a guy for several months just to prove I was over him, but I wasn't in the slightest." She punched me in the arm. "Fine. You can use me and try to make her jealous."

"I'm not trying to make her jealous." I barked out a laugh. "I just want to show her that I'm okay and moving on."

She threw her head back and laughed. "You are so full of shit, Ethan. I'll go with you because I really don't want to sit around here for four days alone, but we will talk about this whole making her jealous thing later."

"Great. It will be fun."

"Oh, I'm sure it will be."

After Sam went back to her room, I wondered if that invite had been a mistake. But then I realized that I had to move on, and Riley needed to see that I had.

What really sucked was that Riley was still right there in the center of my mind and heart, no matter what I tried.

CHAPTER ELEVEN

RILEY

The day after Rebecca and I talked, I stood in my kitchen and dwelled over our conversation. Ethan would be back tomorrow, and what would he say? Was it even right to tell him about the baby when he was about to learn that his mother was dying?

I was a selfish person, I knew that, but wasn't that just a little bit too selfish? Perhaps I would wait until after the funeral and then tell him. Maybe it would lift his spirits.

I clenched my eyes—or make him even more upset than he already was. Was there ever a good time to announce you were pregnant? Maybe for a lot of couples, but Ethan and I weren't a couple.

Coral had told me at the coffee shop yesterday that Ethan was bringing a woman home with him. A woman! He'd been gone for four weeks and had already found another woman to warm his bed. What was he going to do when I told him he was going to be a father? What would the woman say? Was it serious with them?

I wouldn't admit it to anyone, but I missed Ethan every moment of the day. It was like the minute he was gone, he was all I could think about. Now he had someone new in his life. I had screwed all of this up so badly.

I knew that Rebecca was keeping my secret. Had my family heard of my pregnancy, they would have been banging down my door. I was glad they didn't know because I was still trying to wrap my mind around the changes my life was about to undergo.

It wasn't that I hadn't wanted children. I thought kids were great. I just hadn't planned to have one this soon. In hindsight, I guess I figured I had a couple more years before I needed to give it serious thought, and during that time, I would find a man that I loved and wanted to spend my life with.

I stared at my back window as I held my coffee cup in my hands. Now I was going to be a single mother. Ethan had moved on and probably wouldn't want anything to do with me. I had no clue how his new career would affect him when it came to the baby. Would he look at it as a good thing or bad? Obviously, with me attached to it, it would be bad.

What if he had a baby with this other woman? Then our baby would have a half-sibling. I didn't want our baby to have a half-sibling. Was that weird?

Was that because I wanted Ethan to myself? I'd never considered a serious relationship with him. Would he break up with the other woman when he knew I was carrying his child?

I winced. I didn't want him to be with me just because I was having a baby. I wasn't even sure that I wanted to be with him. A little voice inside my mind whispered, *of course, you do*.

I set down my coffee without even taking a sip. I had learned the other day that I could smell the coffee all I wanted, but drinking it turned my stomach upside down until about two in the afternoon. I wanted to be irritated, but I couldn't.

My hand floated to my belly, and I sighed. What kind of a life could I give this little one? Yes, I had a stable job, but I sucked at relationships, and I wasn't committed to anything besides having fun. Not that I'd had much of that in the last several weeks. Nope, I'd been sober as a stone.

I also didn't know what to tell Joe. I was still seeing him, and we'd gone out at least once a week, but I'd always put the brakes on sleeping with him. It wasn't that I didn't want to. I just didn't think it was fair to sleep with him while carrying another man's baby—especially if he didn't know.

I knew that we were both on the cusp of becoming more emotionally invested in our relationship. I think that if I gave Joe the encouragement he was looking for, we'd take the next step. Sadly, that step involved me telling the truth, and I wasn't quite ready for that.

For some reason, I didn't want to tell him before I told Ethan. It only made sense to let the father know before anyone else knew, right?

I wished that I had someone to talk about all of this with, but I couldn't say anything to my family. I sure couldn't say anything to anyone else in his family. All of my friends were friends with either his or my family. God! Why did I have to live in such a small town?

There was a knock on my door, and then it opened. "Hey, your door is unlocked," Henley said as he came in.

"Yeah, so?"

"So, you should keep it locked. You never know when some crazy person is going to come in."

"Like you?" I said to him and quickly poured my coffee down the drain so he wouldn't ask me why I wasn't drinking it.

"Funny, no, but you should lock your door."

"I guess I forgot when I got home last night."

He grinned. "Joe keeping you up late?"

I wish, I wanted to reply. "I'm not sleeping with Joe."

"Say what?" He laughed. "You've been with the guy for like a month."

"So?"

"So, when have you ever dated someone that long and not been sleeping with them? Does he suck in bed? I could give him some tips."

"That's gross, Hen!" I snapped at him. "I'm not talking to you about this. What are you doing here?"

"Coming to see if you were going to make it to the Winstons this weekend. They are having a picnic on Sunday."

"Of course, I'll be there."

"You going to bring Joe?"

"I don't know." I shrugged. "I'll see if he wants to come."

"You should. You should invite his kids too. It would be nice to have more kids around. Then maybe Mom would get off my back about Roxy and me having a baby." He grinned at me. "Besides, it will be good practice for you."

I went utterly still. Did Hen somehow know? "What are you talking about?"

"Well, you keep this up with Joe, and you might just have a couple of stepkids."

I hoped that he couldn't see the relief wash over my face. "Funny." I gave him a fake smile, and as I turned away, I paused and spun back. "Hen, do you think I'd be a good mother?"

He laughed for a moment. "Yeah, I guess, but you'd have to get used to someone else being the center of attention."

"Am I really that bad?" Ethan had said something about me being spoiled, but was I that bad?

Henley took me by the shoulders. "Ry, you put every other woman I know to shame."

I pursed my lips and felt tears start to well up in my eyes. Henley saw them before I could even attempt to stop them.

"Hey! What's with the tears? Where is your snarky comment or rude comeback?"

"What do I do that makes everyone think I am so spoiled?" I almost stomped my foot, but I stopped myself. Even I knew that wouldn't have helped my case any.

Henley laughed, but it ended quickly, and a confused look passed over his face. "Ry, you are rather needy, but that doesn't mean you aren't a good person. You just seem to have to be the center of attention. Plus, you drink way too much, and you sleep with a lot of guys."

"No, I don't! I'll have you know that I haven't had one drink in four weeks!"

He blinked and stepped back. "You haven't? Why?"

"Because I'm trying to show you all that I don't have to drink to have fun. Ethan was on this huge kick when he left about me being an alcoholic, but I'm not!" I shouted and swiped at a tear on my face. "I'm not a drunk, and I'm going to show him and all of you that I'm not."

I put my face into my hands and started to sob. These stupid hormones made me cry at everything, and I hated losing control. Henley probably thought I'd lost my mind.

"Hey, Riley, what's going on?" He pulled me into his arms. "What is this all about?"

"Nothing," I mumbled into his chest.

"You forget how close we are. I know you are upset about something. What is it? Tell me what's going on. Did you and Joe have a fight?"

"No," I mumbled.

"Did you have another fight with Ethan?" he asked, and I pushed back from him.

"No! I haven't spoken to him since he left."

"Have you tried to reach out to him?"

"No! I saw him the night before he left." I swiped at my cheeks and turned away from him. "I went over to apologize to him, and he pretty much told me to get lost and that he didn't want to have anything to do with me ever again."

He took me by the shoulders and turned me to face him. "Come on, you gotta cut the guy some slack. He told you he loved you, and you didn't give it back to him. He knows you will never love him, and he needs to put some space between you guys. You can't blame him for being hurt."

"What about me?" I snapped back, and he raised a brow.

"Remember when you asked about being selfish? That right there is selfish. Ethan is allowed to live his own life. You can't hold him back. This training is good for him because it is giving him a chance to get over you. Do you know how hard it was for him to see you with all these other men when he wants you so bad? I can't even imagine how difficult it would be if Roxy didn't love me as I did her. It would be like a constant stab in the gut."

"I do love him, Henley."

"I'm not talking about the love you have for a brother or a friend, Riley. I'm talking about that love deep down inside your gut. That love that takes your breath away when you feel it pulled away from you. The kind of love that makes your life worthless unless they are in it."

I opened my mouth to say that I felt that for Ethan, but did I? I couldn't remember a time that I felt it in my gut—except these last four weeks. Was that the pregnancy or my feelings for Ethan?

"Someday, you are going to look at a man and know that no matter what happens, you would do anything for them. You would give them anything, sacrifice everything you have to have them in your life. When you feel that, then you'll know that you love them. Then you will know that it's right."

"Is that how you felt with Roxy?"

"Yes. That is precisely how I felt with Roxy. I could not imagine a life without her right beside me. I couldn't even imagine having another woman in my bed. It was Roxy or nothing."

I smiled sadly at him. "I'm glad that you have her."

"You'll find someone, Riley. I promise your time will come."

He gave me another hug and then left, telling me he'd see me later. I curled up on the couch and turned on the television. The only thing I had planned today was to watch stupid movies, eat popcorn, and cry.

I WAS UP EARLY on Saturday and was glad that my morning sickness had started to lessen slightly. I had a busy day, as I was going to the store for Rebecca and then cooking for them. I had every intention of getting it done and being gone before Ethan showed up later this afternoon. The last thing I needed was to run into him with his new woman without a huge buffer of people around us.

I hit the store, gathered everything on the list needed, and headed to the house. Rebecca was seated at the table, her coloring off. "How are you feeling, Rebecca?"

She smiled at me. "Not so well today, Riley. Can you help me get to the couch?"

"Absolutely." I helped her get up, and we shuffled to the living room. Her energy was seriously lagging, and she was breathing hard as we finally got to the couch. I helped her lie down and spread a blanket over her.

She put her hand out to my belly as I leaned over her. "You take good care of my grandbaby."

I covered her hand and held it tightly against my stomach as I sat. "I will, I promise."

"And you'll make sure you tell them lots of stories about me, right?"

It was taking everything in me not to break down and sob as I nodded. "Of course, I will, Rebecca."

"Never let my children forget I loved them."

Tears prickled my eyes. "They know, Rebecca. They know."

She smiled and then sighed as she closed her eyes. "Can you go get Richard for me?"

"Absolutely, I'll be right back."

I patted her hand and studied her face. Her color was really off. I quickly headed outside where Richard was in the back shed working on some lawn equipment. "Richard, Rebecca asked for you."

"Alright," he called over his shoulder. "I'll be there in a few."

I twisted my hands. "Richard, I think you need to come now."

He turned and looked at me. Maybe my face showed my concern, or perhaps it was my voice, but he grabbed a rag and began wiping his hands as he rushed to the back door.

I followed him into the house and then to the living room. "Rebecca, you needed me."

There was silence, and Richard went to his knees. "Rebecca? Rebecca, sweetheart, don't go. Not yet, please don't leave me yet."

My hand flew to my mouth, and I turned as the tears exploded from my eyes. No! Not before he got here! I rushed to get my cellphone and hit my brother's number.

"Henley, get to the Winstons' immediately! It's Rebecca." I couldn't say another word and hung up the phone. I heard Richard's deep soulful sobs in the other room, and I put my face in my hands and cried.

CHAPTER TWELVE

ETHAN

$\mathcal{J}$ stretched her hands toward the headboard. "What were you going to say?" I whispered before I kissed her neck.

She giggled. "I was going to say that I was hungry."

I kissed my way up the column of her neck to her chin and over to her mouth. "What? I'm not enough?"

Sam took hold of my face and stared at me. "Oh, you are enough for pleasure, but I have worked up an appetite."

My phone began to ring, and I winked at her before rolling off of her. "You're lucky."

Sam and I had stayed a hotel last night after people in our class started making comments about us spending so much time together. I sat on the side of the hotel bed and saw Cara's number on my screen. "Hey, what's up, sis?"

"Hey, Ethan, you are still coming home today, right?" she asked, sounding serious.

"Yeah, what's going on?"

"Just checking to see what time."

I glanced at my watch. "I'll be heading to the airport in a few minutes. What's going on? You sound upset."

"It's nothing. I'll tell you about it when you get here. When you get in, just come straight over to Mom and Dad's." Did her voice just catch in her throat? "Have a safe flight. I love you, Ethan."

I frowned. "I love you too, Cara. I'll see you this afternoon. You sure you don't want to tell me what's going on?"

"It is nothing that won't wait. I'll see you later. Let me know when you've landed."

"Alright, I will." She disconnected before I could say anything else, and I scowled at the phone.

"Something wrong?" Sam asked from the other side of the bed.

"I don't know. My sister is upset about something but didn't want to talk about it over the phone. She wants us to come to my parents' house as soon as we get in."

She leaned up on her elbow. "You sure you still want me to come?"

"Of course. I'm sure it's nothing. Coral or Candy probably did something stupid, and we are going to have a family meeting about it, or maybe Evan decided to follow his girl-friend across the US after all." I glanced at my watch again. "We should probably shower and head to the airport. If we get checked in early enough, we can grab a decent lunch before the flight."

As we got dressed and headed to the airport, I felt a sense of unease fill my gut. Cara was always cool. She handled pressure like it was just another walk in the park. Something bad happened at home to shake her. Had something happened to Riley?

A sense of panic began to fill me, and I shifted in my seat. The hotel shuttle was taking us from the hotel to the airport, and I suddenly felt that I needed to move. Shit! What if some-thing happened to Riley?

No, if something serious had happened, Cara would have

told me—right? Whatever this was, it wasn't that important. I was not going to stress over it.

I glanced at Sam. I liked her. I really liked the fact that we had no emotions and no strings. She had her life in New York, and I had no intention of leaving mine anytime soon.

I could see Sam and I being friends for years, and I was glad that things were as easy as they were with her. She'd told me all about her husband and her past boyfriend, and I had shared the drama with Riley. Maybe if things were different and we were living closer, it could have been more, but what we had was good.

I smiled at her, thankful for her friendship. I had a feeling I might be leaning on that friendship quite a bit in the next few hours.

I WAS LOOKING FORWARD to a home-cooked meal, especially after our long day. We were supposed to land at three but didn't get in until after five. By the time we got our luggage and the rental car, it was almost six.

Cara had sent me several messages while my phone was off. As soon as I saw them, that uneasy feeling began to slip through my veins again. I told her we were finally on our way.

An hour later, we pulled down the driveway to my parents'. "Shit," I muttered as I took in all the cars.

"Wow, that's a lot of cars."

I blew out a breath. "You know how I told you we were close to the Youngs? Well, it looks like they are here too."

"Oh, does that mean that Riley will be here?"

I glanced over the cars and pointed to one near the house. "Yeah, that's her SUV."

"How do you want to play this?"

"What do you mean?" I asked her as I parked.

"Do you want me to pretend to be your girlfriend or a friend that's a girl?"

I chuckled. "How about we just be us. Don't try to be different. Riley's a big girl; she has seen me with other women, and I have seen her with a ton of men, so it's no big deal."

"Sounds good," she said with a laugh, and we climbed out and took the steps up to the front door.

I expected there to be a lot of noise when we stepped in, but it was oddly quiet for the number of people in the room. My eyes skimmed the room, and I saw nothing but somber faces.

"What the hell is going on?" I asked as I stopped at the edge of the room. "You all look like someone died."

Cara was the first to approach me, and she threw her arms around my neck and started to cry. "Cara, what is going on?"

I scanned the room, my siblings and father were seated around the room. Huntley, Wesley, Patricia, David, and even Kayley were here. Where were my mom, Riley, and Henley?

"It's Mom," Candy said as she stood beside me, tears filling her eyes and sliding down.

"What's wrong with Mom?"

"Ethan," Evan started to speak, but he winced and looked away, turning to Carmen, whose eyes were completely bloodshot.

"Mom died this morning," Candy finally said.

On the other side of the room, Wesley and Hunt sat on either side of their parents. Brad stood in the corner, and they all looked almost as torn to shreds as my siblings. I searched for my father. He was sitting in his favorite chair, staring at the floor.

"Dad?" I pushed away from my sister and went to him. "Dad." I dropped to my knees in front of him.

His eyes were watery, but somehow he held the tears back. "We were gonna tell you all tonight that your momma was sick." He swallowed as if he were struggling. "Her poor body was riddled with cancer, but she didn't even make it for you all to say goodbye. I'm so sorry, son."

I pulled my father into my arms, and the tears began to slide down. How could my momma be dead? It wasn't possible. My father cried with me, and when I pulled back, I saw Riley and Henley standing in the corner. Hen had his arm over her shoulders, and she looked like she had been crying—a lot.

I wanted to go to her, wanted to throw myself into her arms, but I didn't. Suddenly, I remembered Sam had come with me, and I looked back at the door, searching for Sam. Candy said softly that she had gone outside.

I hugged my siblings, taking little comfort in it at the moment. I was numb, unsure of what I should be doing or saying, or fucking feeling! Wes got up and hugged me tightly, and I fought to keep control. My eyes shot to where Riley had been standing, but she was gone. Henley approached me. "She went fast." For a second, I wasn't sure who he was talking about. "Riley was with her, well, sort of. She had been with her, and your mom asked her to get your father. While Riley was gone to get him, she slipped away."

I put my arms around him and cried for a moment as I absorbed the story. Why had Riley been here?

Finally, I pulled back from Henley, and Patricia Young came to me. "My dear son, I am so very sorry, sweetheart. Your mother was such a wonderful person."

I bent down to hug her, and suddenly, I wanted to run from the room. I had come home to take a break from stress and a challenging class. I thought it would be a fun weekend, but it was going to be anything but.

"When did this happen?" I asked anyone who would speak to me.

Henley spoke up. "Around eleven this morning."

Cara had called me at eleven-thirty. She had already known. She should have told me, but maybe it was better that she hadn't. I couldn't imagine traveling all day after just hearing the news.

I stared at a picture of my parents on the piano and wanted to pinch myself. This couldn't be happening. I turned to my father. "How long have you known she was sick?"

"We learned just last week," he replied softly.

"Bullshit! If her body was full of cancer, you had to know before that."

"Ethan," Cara pleaded. "Calm down. We are all upset; don't shout at Dad."

I felt dizzy and hot, and I needed fresh air. I walked back to the front door and out onto the porch. I leaned my elbow against the pole and closed my eyes as I heard footsteps, and then a moment later, I felt a hand on my back.

"I am so sorry, Ethan." Samantha's voice was soft, sad. "I lost my mom two years ago. It is the hardest thing I have ever had to deal with."

I swallowed the lump in my throat. "I didn't expect this."

She turned me to face her, taking my face in her hands. "I know you didn't. No one ever expects it, even when they know it's coming."

"I'm sorry you had to be here for this."

"I think I might take the car and head back to the airport. I think you need your family right now more than you need me. I'll let them know back at school what's going on."

"Fuck!" I growled. "I don't even know what to do with that."

"I'll go back and talk to them, and I'll let you know what they say."

"Don't go back tonight. You are as tired as I am. How about I give you my keys and you head over to my house. I can call and have food delivered over there."

"Hey, I saw fast food down the street. Don't worry about me. I'll fend for myself and get comfortable at your place. You take as long as you need, and if you want me to come pick you up later, you let me know."

"I will," I told her.

She leaned forward and kissed me softly. "I really am sorry, Ethan. It's the worst fucking thing in the world."

When I looked at her, her eyes were glassy, as if she were fighting tears. I pulled her into my arms, needing the feel of someone against me. I was glad that she was here, but also sorry she had to see all this—especially since she had lost her mother recently.

I watched her leave, and then I stood there for a few moments. I heard footsteps off to my side and turned to find Riley coming around the side of the house.

"Oh, I'm sorry. I didn't mean to disturb you," she said softly and looked away.

"It's okay. I was just thinking." She nodded and began to move toward her car. "Where are you going?"

She paused, turning back. "I'm not feeling so great. It's been a long day, and I just want to go home." I studied her. She did look tired, and her face looked a little puffy like she'd gained a few pounds. "I'm sorry you had to come home to this," she said softly and then began to turn again.

"Riley, wait!" I started to take the stairs down toward her, but she held her hand up.

"You really shouldn't get close to me, Ethan. You don't want to catch what I have."

"I'm not going to, Ry," I told her, suddenly needing to have her in my arms. Of everyone here, it was her that I wanted to seek solace with the most.

"I'm so sorry about your mom, Ethan. Go be with your family. I'm sure I'll see you before you leave again."

She didn't give me a choice as she rushed off to get in her SUV and took off down the driveway like demons were chasing her.

CHAPTER THIRTEEN

RILEY

*T*oday had been a living nightmare. Being there with Richard after Rebecca passed was overwhelming, but then my brother arrived, and he quickly took over. He called Cara and then my parents. He was going to leave it up to Cara to inform her siblings.

When Cara arrived, she had quickly decided that they would not tell Ethan until he came home this afternoon. She knew how hard it would be on him and didn't want him to deal with that while traveling. What were a few hours?

My mother, Henley, and I worked in the kitchen. We made sure there was plenty to eat for everyone as they arrived. Daniella, Roxy, and Charlotte were here earlier in the day but left before Ethan showed up. They said tonight it should just be our two families.

Henley and I were in the kitchen cleaning dishes when the front door opened and I heard Ethan's voice. Hen and I looked at one another, and he pulled me into his arm for a moment. The tears started immediately again. It was going to be hard enough seeing him again after the way we had parted, but knowing he was coming home to this. I could not imagine his pain.

Ethan was on his knees in front of his father when Henley and I joined the front room. His cries tore at my soul, and I wanted to gather him to me, but I held back. His gaze collided with mine, and the disbelief was so stark that it took the air from my lungs.

I didn't see the woman he was supposed to be bringing home; maybe she didn't come, but then I heard his sister talking about someone going outside. I slipped out of the room before making a fool of myself and throwing myself into his arms.

Henley followed me into the kitchen. "You okay?"

"Yeah, I'm just tired, Henley. It's been such a long day."

"You look tired, Riley. Why don't you go home? You've done a lot today." He paused. "Why were you here in the first place?"

I glanced at the door to the front room. "I knew she was sick. I had been coming over to help her and Richard."

"Why didn't you say anything?"

"Because they didn't want anyone to know. They were going to tell all the kids today when Ethan came home."

"Damn," he muttered. "Okay, go get some rest. I'm sure you'll have time to speak to Ethan later."

Ha! Like I was ready to have a conversation with him? I slipped out the back door, and as I got to the front corner of the house, I paused when I heard voices. I peered around the corner and saw a woman in Ethan's arms. They were too far away for me to make out what they were saying, but it was obvious that they were intimate as she kissed him and caressed his face before walking off.

I slipped back behind the house so she wouldn't see me as she left and hoped that he would have gone inside by the time I headed to my car—no such luck.

Ethan started approaching me, and I fled. I couldn't be near him right now. My heart was so heavy, and my emotions were such a mess that I knew if he touched me, I would fall to pieces and confess everything. Tonight was not the right time.

I hated myself as I got in my vehicle and left. I had seen the need in his eyes, but I couldn't give him that. I couldn't be what he needed, not when I didn't know what I wanted or needed from him.

My god, I *was* selfish.

I drove home, hating myself, and went right to the shower where I cried again for like the hundredth time today. My face was puffy and the skin under my eyes chapped from all the salty tears I'd shed.

I lay down and within seconds fell into a deep slumber of exhaustion. I woke at nine the next morning and crawled out of bed to use the bathroom. When I finally got down to the kitchen, I poured a big glass of orange juice before locating my phone on the counter.

I had a few text messages, but nothing urgent. Coral thanked me for all I had done. Henley and my mom were checking on me. I replied to them and wondered what was next. The picnic planned for the day was off, and I wasn't sure what I should be doing with myself.

As I thought about it, I had this undeniable urge to see my parents. I showered and headed over to their house. I guess I wasn't the only one who needed to be close to our parents because Wesley and Charlotte were there with Marisol. Brad and his kids were there, and Huntley was also parked in the kitchen.

Kayley and Daniella were cooking when I walked in. Kayley had come home from New York as soon as my mother called her yesterday. There wasn't one of us who didn't feel Rebecca's loss almost as strongly as her own children.

There were times when I was growing up that I'd been more comfortable telling Rebecca about things than I was my own mother. She had always given me good advice.

"Where is Henley?" I asked after I'd hugged my parents tightly.

"Both he and Roxy have to work today," my father said as he pulled me to his side and kept his arm around my shoulders.

"Ah, I thought they had the day off for the picnic."

"No, Henley had to work; Roxy got called in for an emergency. She'll be here in a little while," Hunt stated.

"Well, since we have most of you here, your mother and I want to say something."

Brad glared at my father as the rest of us looked around nervously. "Don't you dare say one of you is terminally sick," Brad growled.

"No, we are fine, but we wanted to tell you how much we appreciate how quickly you all responded to help yesterday. I know you have been close to them for years, but I think you all being there for them yesterday was helpful. If something happened to one of us, I imagine that they would do the same for us."

My mother stepped next to me. "They are going to continue to need us. I know the kids didn't know about her illness, but Riley and I did. Riley was with her right before she passed, and the two of us had spent a lot of time with her and Richard this week to help them as needed."

"How did you two know?" Kayley asked.

"I saw them coming out of the doctors, and they looked like their world had been turned upside down. I went over to see them, and Richard told me. He said I could tell Mom, but he didn't want anyone else to know until they could tell the kids all at once."

"You know, I would be pretty pissed if I knew that one of you were dying and you weren't telling us," Hunt stated roughly. "They missed out on a couple of days with their mother."

"She didn't want them to know," I stated. "She didn't want them to change their life just because she was dying."

"Still, don't do that shit to us," Hunt said. "If one of you are dying, I want to know."

"Okay, Hunt," my father said to calm him. "We will do that."

"I have a better idea," Wesley said. "Don't die anytime soon."

"Oh, Wes, you know as well as we do that life is precious. You have to enjoy every moment of every day. You need to love the people you are with and be with the ones you love." My mother looked at me pointedly.

"What? I hang out with you all as much as I can."

Huntley laughed. "She's not talking about us, Ry. She's talking about you and Ethan."

"Stop!" I threw my hand up as I stepped away from my parents. "Do not start on me with Ethan, please. I know I need to speak with him, and I need to apologize, but right now is not the time to do that. Especially when he brought home his girlfriend."

"That's not his girlfriend," Brad said.

"Oh, it's not, huh? Then why was she kissing him outside?"

Huntley laughed. "What were you doing, spying on them?"

"No!" I crossed my arms over my chest. "I was leaving and saw them. I don't care whether that's his girlfriend or not. Nothing like that matters right now."

"He told me that she was just a classmate that didn't have any place to go on break," Brad stated.

"Well, good for them," I stated.

Huntley got up and headed to the coffee pot, stopping to shove my arm as he laughed. "Look at the jealousy on your face."

I turned and punched him in the shoulder. "I am not jealous!" Everyone laughed. "I'm not jealous!" I announced to the room loudly before I stomped my foot and then rushed from the room.

After our late breakfast, I had gone home and was lying on the couch. As I flipped channels, I idly wondered what to do with the rest of my day and tried to find a movie to get lost in when someone knocked on my door. I sighed as I got up to answer it. Maybe it would be a vacuum cleaner salesperson, and they could keep me company for a little while.

I opened it to find not a stranger, but Roxy, Daniella, and Charlotte. "Can we come in?" Charlotte grinned, holding up a bottle of wine.

I held the door open. "What are you guys doing here?"

"Well, we thought we'd crack open a bottle of wine and try to get you to tell us what's wrong."

"Um, Rebecca just died."

Roxy rolled her eyes. "We know you are upset about that. We are trying to figure out what else is bothering you."

"Nothing is bothering me," I said as Charlotte went into my kitchen and dug around in my drawer for the corkscrew. Damn, how was I going to get out of this?

Roxy pulled down four glasses, and Daniella went to take a seat on the couch, asking, "Is it Joe or Ethan?"

I stared at her. "Is what Joe or Ethan?"

"Is what is getting you down related to Joe or Ethan?" Roxy asked as she carried a wineglass to me. I stared at the glass and then took it from her.

"Neither," I said as I sat down on the other end of the couch from Daniella.

"Alright, so how are things with Joe?" Charlotte said as she handed Daniella her wine and sat in the chair across from me.

"Fine, I guess."

Roxy cocked her head. "Fine, you guess? Girl, that man is gorgeous! You have to share a bit more here."

I laughed a little uncomfortably. "Well, I only see him once a week. We're keeping it pretty low-key because of the kids."

"Is he good in bed?" Charlotte asked with a giggle.

"I honestly have no idea. We have not slept together."

Her jaw dropped, and Roxy threw her arm out as she pulled

her wineglass from her mouth. "Wait! You haven't slept with that man? Why the hell not?"

"Um, because I said we were taking it slow."

Charlotte was observing me way too carefully. I avoided her gaze. I put the wineglass to my lips as if I were taking a sip, but I didn't.

"So is that why you are all emotional recently? No sexual release?" Roxy asked.

I forced a loud laugh. "Guys, come on. It's been a hectic few weeks." I set the wineglass down and fluffed a pillow.

Charlotte leaned forward. "So, if you haven't slept with Joe, the baby is Ethan's then, right?"

I froze for a second too long. "What are you talking about?"

Daniella yelped. "Wait! You're pregnant? Oh, my god! That makes so much sense now!"

My mind spun, and the words to deny it wouldn't come out.

"Holy crap, Riley." Roxy pulled her hand from her mouth. "Are you really pregnant?"

I put my hands to the sides of my head and leaned forward. Charlotte came to my side, rubbing her hand down my back. "I recognized all the signs."

"What signs?"

"Not feeling well, losing weight, then gaining it again, the circles under your eyes, the ability to cry at the drop of a hat, and the fact that you never wanted to leave your house. You not gulping your wine was just the final clue for me."

I lifted my face, a few stray tears running down my cheeks. "You guys can't tell anyone! I'm serious! You can't tell my brothers!"

"That's why you haven't slept with Joe," Daniella stated.

"Yes, that's why. As much as I wanted to, I couldn't do that when I was carrying someone else's child."

"Ethan doesn't know, does he?"

I shook my head as I wiped at my face. "No, I literally found out the day before he left for training. I was going to tell him about it this weekend, but then his mother passed, and I can't do that to him."

"Do what? Give him hope?" Roxy asked.

"Hope for what?" I asked her.

"For a family. For the two of you to finally settle down."

"Whoa! First off, I'm not sure if you noticed, but Ethan moved on. He told me before he left that he didn't want anything to do with me. Second, I'm not sure I want to settle down and have a family."

"Ethan said that because he was mad and trying to put distance between you. He's not going to want that now. How far along are you?"

"Eight and a half weeks."

"Riley." Charlotte took my hand. "You need to tell Ethan."

"How can I do that when he's dealing with the loss of his mother? How can I tell him when he has another woman with him?"

"Huntley told me that Sam was flying back to Georgia today. She's not here anymore. If those two were so close, do you think she would have left him?" Daniella asked. "God knows that if I cared about someone and they lost a parent, there is no way I would leave them. None of us would."

"You need to go talk to him, Riley," Roxy said.

"And say what? I'm sorry your mom died, but hey, guess what, we're having a baby?"

They all looked at one another, and then Charlotte shrugged. "Well, yeah."

CHAPTER FOURTEEN

ETHAN

*T*he shock was wearing off, and I was sitting on the front porch staring out into the darkness. All of us were here at the house, well, all except Mom. None of us wanted to go home—none of us wanted to leave Dad.

What kind of world would it be without my mom in it anymore? Cara was seated in the glider beside me, Evan on her other side. Carmen, Candy, and Coral were inside doing something with Dad.

Cara sighed, and the sound was heavy in the night air.

"You had no idea, Cara? They never told you?"

"No." She shook her head. "I had no clue. I think the only ones who knew besides her and Dad were Riley and her mother."

"Why did they know?"

"I don't know. I haven't wanted to push Dad to talk too much yet."

"Jesus, if Riley knew, she should have told me," I muttered back.

Cara snorted. "Like you two are talking these days. I noticed that she bolted right after you arrived. Did you even talk to her?"

"For a moment, she said she was tired. She looked it, too."

"She's the one that called the ambulance. Henley is the one that pronounced Mom."

"Shit." I rubbed my forehead. I had a massive headache.

"So what's up with this Sam girl you brought back?" Evan asked.

"She's just a classmate. She called a little while ago to say she got an early flight back to Georgia. She's going to let me know what they say when she gets back."

"Why did she come up here in the first place?" Cara queried.

"Because she didn't have anyplace else to go," I replied.

Cara frowned. "She doesn't have a home?"

"What's with all the questions?"

Cara shrugged. "Just weird that you bring a woman home with you."

I laughed. "Why is that so weird? I've brought other women around that I have dated."

Evan grinned. "So you *are* dating her?"

"No, I didn't say that." I sighed heavily. "Sam and I have an arrangement."

"You're using each other for sex," Cara stated with a raised brow.

"Yeah, what's wrong with that?"

She snorted. "Ethan, when are you going to learn that you can't do that to avoid feelings? Your relationship with Riley started that way too, but look how that turned out."

"Riley and I don't have a relationship," I stated harshly.

"I think she missed you while you were gone," Evan added.

"I doubt that very much, but why would you think that?"

"Because she was never out at the tavern. You know she always went out on Thursday nights, but she hasn't been out once since you left."

"What are you doing, stalking her, Ev?"

He laughed. "Hardly. I figured that since I was always there on Thursday nights, I would make sure she got home safe since you weren't around."

"Why are we even talking about her? I don't want to talk about Riley."

"Okay, then tell us more about Sam," Cara said sweetly.

"No. My love life is off the table. How about we talk about something that matters. Like when are we going to have Mom's funeral?"

The minute the words were out of my mouth, I wanted to take them back. For just a few moments, I had forgotten that my mom was gone. I was pretty sure by the looks on their faces that they also had.

"Brad called the funeral home for me today," Cara said softly. "Because of the holiday and your schedule, it's kind of tricky."

"I don't care about my schedule," I snapped. "I'll miss the damn class. I don't care."

"Ethan, Mom would not want you to do that. I was going to say that Saturday is our best bet anyway, so you can head back to class and then come back on Friday night."

"You want me to go back for three days and then fly back?"

"Yes," she stated forcefully. "Mom would want you to do that. Hell, Mom would expect you to. You know she never wanted to be a burden to us. Never wanted to interrupt our lives."

Suddenly, Cara's face screwed up, and she put her hands to her face and started sobbing. I hung my head as Evan put his arm around her and pulled her toward him.

"I've been so busy. We've all been so busy." She looked at Evan. "When was the last time you came by to visit?"

He frowned. "I guess it's been three weeks—shit."

"Yeah, well, I hadn't seen her since before I went to training," I announced, and Cara spun on me as she wiped her cheeks.

"Yeah, but you had a reason! You were a thousand miles

away, Ethan. It's not like you could just pop on over to say hello or share a cup of coffee or dinner. I could have, but I didn't." She batted tears away with the backs of her hands. "I could have, but I was always busy! All of us were!"

"Enough!" my father's voice roared from the door. "Your mother would be beside herself hearing this discussion," he said as he came out onto the porch, my other siblings behind him. "Your mother did not want you to know because of this. Because she knew that the moment you all knew, you would stop your lives and hover over her. She did not want any of you to put your lives on hold."

"Come on, Dad. Putting our lives on the back burner for a few days or weeks is nothing compared to what she gave us. What you both gave us growing up," I told him. "Both of you deserve every minute of our time that you want. All you have to do is ask. Shit! You shouldn't even have to ask. That's it, I'm not going back to class, and I'm going to leave county detectives and come back to Millerstown."

"The hell you will, young man," my father growled. "Do not even let me hear such foolishness come out of your mouth. Your mother is proud of every single one of you." He glanced around the porch. "She loved you all so much, you were her life, and she was happy when she knew you were busy. It was when you were always calling her, crying on her shoulder, confused about where life was taking you that she worried about you. She did not want to tell you because she wanted to remember you all the way you are, not staring down at her with fear and sadness, and she sure as hell did not want you to see her suffer."

He shook his head as Carmen put her arm around his waist and leaned into him. "I thank the Lord that he took your mother before you all were here. Yes, I am heartbroken, and I will miss her until my last breath, but I am glad that she went as quickly as she did and as peacefully. She was loved and happy in her last few moments." He stared at me hard as he spoke the last line. "All of you need to remember that. Your mother died the way she lived —exactly how she wanted to. Now, you guys can sit around here and mourn for a few days, and then you are going to get back to your life. We all will." He lifted his chin, his strength radiating out of him. I had no clue where he was finding that strength just then.

He stepped toward me, putting his hand on my arm. "Son, you will go back to your class, and we'll wait to hear from you when you can get back up here for the funeral. Your class is essential to your career. Your momma believed in you, as I do. You will finish that class."

"Yes, sir." I nodded, and he squeezed and let go.

"And the rest of you, I don't expect you to change your entire life because I am alone now. I'll get by. I'll be fine."

"Oh, right, Dad," Carmen said. "I can't remember the last time you cooked."

Candy laughed. "Or did the laundry."

My father cracked a smile. "Okay, so maybe you all can change your routines a little bit to help me get it all figured out." He spun around and pointed at me. "Except you. You are staying right where you are until you finish. Then we will talk when you come home."

"Okay, Dad," I told him with a smile. Whatever the man wanted, I'd give him.

SUNDAY WAS THE FOURTH, and instead of the big picnic we had planned, we had a small family dinner. Even the Youngs gave us space, and we played a few games, talked about what to do with some of Mom's things, and helped Dad look through paper-work to find life insurance and other vital documents.

On Monday, we visited the funeral home and made arrangements. It was one of the hardest things I had ever had to do. I wasn't sure how my father was still standing upright.

The funeral would be the following Saturday afternoon. I'd already talked to my instructors and told them that I was coming back to training but would need to leave a little early on Friday to make my flight back. They told me I could drop out of the class and step into the next one, but my father probably would have knocked me out if I'd done that. He was right. I needed to finish what I started—as hard as it would be to be away from family right now.

On Tuesday morning, I checked to make sure that everything was off in my house before I left for the airport. I was driving myself since I would be back in a few days. It was easier for me to do that than have someone come down to pick me up.

I was just about to leave when there was a soft knock at the door. I pulled the door open and startled back. I hadn't seen Riley since Saturday night. "Riley."

"Ethan," she said as she wrung her hands. "Can we talk?"

I exhaled loudly through my nose but stepped back to hold the door open. "I only have a few minutes before I have to leave."

"You're leaving?" She seemed surprised as she crossed the threshold. That wasn't all she appeared either. She looked exhausted.

"Yeah, I need to go back to class, but I'll be back on Friday night for the weekend."

"Oh, well, I should let you go. Maybe we can talk then." She turned back to the door, and suddenly I needed her to stay. I stepped into her path, her surprised eyes flashing to mine.

"You were with my mom when she died. Why?"

Riley shuffled back slightly. "I was trying to help. I knew that everyone would be there that afternoon. My mother and I were cooking for the picnic so that your mom didn't get worn out."

"What did she say to you before she died?"

"Um…" She looked away and gnawed on her bottom lip for a moment. "She asked me to go get your father."

"What else did she say, Riley?"

"Nothing." I knew Riley well enough to know that she was hiding something. I stepped forward, and she moved back until the wall was behind her.

"Riley, I've been in a class for four weeks learning to tell when people lie. I know you aren't telling me something, Riley. What aren't you telling me?"

"It was personal, Ethan. It has nothing to do with you."

"Nothing to do with me?" My voice rose. "You were with my mother for days before she died. Why you? Why not one of her own kids?"

She shook her head, her eyes wide. "I don't know. She didn't want to bother you guys."

"But she bothered you?"

"I'm on summer break," she said quickly.

"Why didn't you call me and tell me?"

"She asked me not to."

"Riley, you knew my mother was sick, that she was dying. You should have called me and told me."

Riley blinked rapidly. "I'm sorry, Ethan. I'm sorry that I didn't call you, but if I had, would you even have answered your phone?"

"What are you talking about?"

She crossed her arms over her chest, and I stepped back slightly to avoid contact with her. "Now that you have a new girlfriend, would you even have answered your phone?"

"New?" I spiked a brow at her and laughed. "Are you referring to yourself as the old one? Because I'm pretty sure that was never a description that you wanted."

She looked away. "I'm sorry. I shouldn't have come here." She started to step around me, but I grabbed her arm.

"Why did you come here?"

"Because I wanted to tell—" She swallowed as her eyes shot off to the side. "I wanted to say I was sorry—for everything, Ethan. I'm sorry about what happened the night you left. I'm sorry for not calling to tell you about your mother, and I'm sorry she's gone."

As I stared at her, I knew there was something she was holding back. "What is it that you aren't telling me, Riley? Things get serious with Joe? Or did you all break up, and you're crawling back to me for one last good time in bed?"

She lifted her face, and there was that rebellious nature that I had fallen in love with—my heart started to race, and I almost grabbed her face and brought her lips to mine.

"The last thing I would ever do is crawl to any man, including you, Ethan Winston." She yanked her arm out of my grasp and pushed her way around me.

She rushed down my front stairs and around the corner, and I sighed. I glanced at my watch and realized I had to get moving, or I was going to miss my flight. I would find a way to talk to her this weekend.

CHAPTER FIFTEEN

RILEY

I had every intention of telling Ethan that he would be a father when I had arrived at his house, but I never got the chance. He was confrontational and slightly bitter right from the start. Was that because I had told him previously that I didn't want a relationship with him? Or was he angry with me for not telling him about his mother?

I rushed to my car and fought the tears the whole way. I should never have listened to them. Roxy, Charlotte, and Daniella had talked me into coming to see him. It had taken two days of urging me, but finally, I had sucked up the fear and shown up on his doorstep.

The sight of him standing there had taken my breath away. I forgot how handsome he was, how beautiful his blue eyes were. I'd forgotten just how tall he was, how I felt almost dwarfed by him at times, but protected too. When he had stalked me to the wall, I'd been tempted to throw myself around him, beg him to forgive me for everything.

But how could I do any of that without telling him that he would be a father? I couldn't, and with the mood that he was in, today was not the right time to do it, either—especially since he had to leave.

It was later that afternoon when Roxy and Henley showed up at my door, and Roxy took one look at me. "Oh, no! What happened?"

I shook my head, glancing at Henley. I could not talk about this in front of my brother.

"Why are you crying?" Henley said, and Roxy winced and mouthed sorry toward me.

"I was thinking about Rebecca," I said as I gave him my back.

"You know, you're almost more upset than her own kids." Henley followed me into the room. "Why?"

I shrugged. "Because I am. Let it go, Henley."

"No, I think there is something else going on." He took a seat, and I watched him as he stared at Roxy. "Wait, you know something. You know why she's upset."

She shook her head dramatically.

"Oh, bullshit!" Henley turned to me. "What's going on? What aren't you two telling me?"

"Nothing, Lee!" I hissed at him and put my face in my hands. "Just let it go."

It was quiet for a minute, and then my brother came to sit beside me. "Riley, what's going on? I know you haven't been yourself for weeks. Ever since Ethan left—" He paused. "Is this because of Ethan? Did you finally realize you were in love with him?"

"No," I said softly.

"But this is about Ethan, right? What's going on? Did you two have another fight?"

I heard the whisper of shoes across the carpet and knew Roxy was coming to sit near us. "Riley, tell your brother."

Oh, my god! I couldn't! Once I said this out loud, it was going to be more true. Henley would freak out, and what would the rest of my family do? I could just hear Henley now, going on about how irresponsible I was.

He put his arm around me. "Riley, whatever it is, it's not so bad. Tell me what's going on. Let me help you. I know that something has been bothering you for weeks, but I was giving you space. I'm not going to do that anymore, and I'm not leaving until you tell me."

"I'm pregnant," I breathed out softly, and it went silent around me, only the sound of my heart thundering in my ears.

"I'm sorry, what did you say?"

I pushed my hair back from my face. "I said I'm pregnant, Henley."

He leaned back from me and stared at me. "You're serious?"

"No, I'd joke about something like that," I growled at him.

"Is this Joe's or Ethan's?"

"I haven't slept with Joe."

"Is it Ethan's or someone else?"

I stared at my brother. "I'm not that much of a skank. It's Ethan's."

"What did he say when you told him?"

I glanced at Roxy. "I haven't told him yet."

Lines marred his brow. "Why the hell not?"

"Because both times that I tried, they haven't been the right times."

He laughed shortly. "You need to make it the right time, Riley. How far along are you?"

"Almost nine weeks."

"Jesus, Riley! When were you going to tell us?"

"After I told Ethan. I was still trying to figure out what I was going to do."

He studied me. "What do you mean, what you were going to do? Do you mean you considered having an abortion?"

"No, not really."

"Not really? Do you know how pissed Ethan would have

been once he found out about that? How pissed all of us would have been?"

"No one would have known."

His laugh was brutal. "Yeah, like anyone can keep a secret in this town."

"Hey! I kept a secret for five weeks! I've known I was pregnant since the night before he left, and no one else except my doctor and his mother knew."

"You told his mother?"

"No, she guessed," I said softly. "I was asking her questions about her life so that I could tell the baby about her, and she guessed."

"Hmm—" He sat for a moment staring at me. "Why didn't you tell Ethan?"

"I was going to tell him the night before he left, but we had a huge fight, and he was going on about how he had to get over me and move on, and I couldn't say it. I was struck mute, and I wished him well and ran out the door. At that point, I wasn't sure what I was doing yet. I had just learned about it myself."

"Did you try to talk to him while he was home this time?"

"Henley, I was going to. That was my plan before Rebecca died. I was going to try and get a few minutes alone with him and tell him, but then he brought that woman with him, and I realized that he moved on. But Roxy, Charlotte, and Daniella figured out what was going on with me, and they talked me into going to see him. I went this morning, but he was getting ready to leave, and he was angry with me—again."

"He was angry with you?"

"Yes, he asked if I had broken up with Joe and was crawling back to him."

Henley's features hardened, and I grabbed his hand. "Henley, you need to stay out of this. I will speak to him. I swear I will do it. I know I need to tell him. It won't be long before I can't hide it anymore anyway."

"Are you okay? I can't believe you kept this to yourself all this time." He pulled me into his arms, leaning back on the couch and pulling me with him. "Jesus, Riley, you should have said something."

"I wasn't ready, and I didn't want you all to look at me as a failure."

He leaned back, lifting my chin so he could see my face. "A failure? Riley, you're going to be a mother. What about being a mother would be a failure? Do you know how freaking happy Mom and Dad are going to be?"

"Don't you dare tell them!"

"I won't, but you better do it soon."

"I will. I need to find time to speak with Ethan next weekend. He'll be back for the funeral, and I hate to spring it on him, but if I don't tell him then, he won't be back until I'm four months pregnant. That would really shock the hell out of him."

"You need to tell him, Riley," my brother stressed. "He has the right to know. Why don't you just call him? It might be easier to do it over the phone."

"Henley, if you and Roxy were at odds, would you want to find out that you were going to be a father over the phone while you were a thousand miles away?"

He stared at Roxy. "Okay, fine, not over the phone, but you are going to tell him next weekend."

"I will. I know I need to."

Henley grinned at me. "My baby sister is going to be a momma."

"Watch it," I said with mock anger.

He pulled me tightly to his chest and laughed as he asked a bunch of questions that I didn't have answers to about a nursery, names, and feedings.

When Roxy and Henley left a few hours later, I felt better than I had in weeks. Of all my siblings, it had been Henley that I had worried the most about telling. Being only eleven months younger than him, we were very close, and I didn't want to disappoint him. I was so glad that I hadn't, or at least he didn't appear to be disappointed. He seemed oddly excited, to be honest.

THE WEEK WENT by in a flash, and before I knew it, it was Friday night. Daniella came over to watch a movie marathon with me since Hunt was working, and she had just finished her most recent manuscript. We pigged out on pretzel bites and popcorn just like if we were at the movies, and it was almost midnight when she left.

I was just turning the lights off when there was a knock at the door, and I yawned and glanced around the living room. She must have forgotten something.

I pulled open the door and froze. Ethan stood on the other side, and he didn't look happy, especially with the red mark on his cheekbone that looked suspiciously like it was going to turn into a bruise at any moment. "What are you doing here?"

"Why didn't you tell me?"

The ground under me shifted, and I clung to the door. "What are you talking about?"

He pushed the door open, and I stumbled back. "Don't play games, Riley. Why didn't you tell me you were pregnant?"

I swallowed. Who had told him? Suddenly, the mark on his face and my brother's image meshed. "Did Henley tell you that?"

"What difference is it who told me? You should have, Riley! If it's even mine."

I glared at him. "Get out!"

"Not until you tell me the truth, Riley. Are you pregnant?"

I shook my hair back from my face and glared at him. "I am."

"Is it mine?"

I ground my teeth and forced myself not to cry. My hand itched to smack his face, but I held myself back. "What if it is?"

"Oh, no, Riley. You are going to tell me the damn truth." He paused. "Unless you don't know if it's mine or not."

"It's your child, Ethan." I spun away from him, needing to put space between us. For a moment, I had wondered if he would try to stop me from moving away, but he seemed rooted to the spot when I glanced at him from the other side of the couch.

"How do I know it's mine?"

"Because I hadn't slept with anyone for about two months before we slept together, and I haven't been with anyone since."

"You expect me to believe that?" he snarled.

"You can believe whatever the hell you want!" I snapped back.

"Why didn't you tell me, Ry?"

"Because both times that I tried, Ethan, you jumped down my throat. I was going to tell you about it before you left. I actually found out the night before, but you were angry with me. You told me you wanted me out of your life. How was I supposed to tell you then? And when you first came back, you were so upset about your mom. I couldn't do it then. But I came over on Tuesday morning, and I was going to tell you, but you got angry with me again, and I couldn't do it."

He shook his head, his eyes raking down my body and back up before he laughed bitterly and put his hand on his hips. "Well, fuck!"

"Look, I don't want anything from you, Ethan. You don't even have to be part of this child's life if you don't want to."

His face turned into a mask of rage. "Are you kidding me? What kind of a man do you think I am, Riley Young? I don't walk out on my responsibilities. You can damn well bet that from this moment on, I will be a part of that baby's life. I want to know every detail about that child, and you do not have any right to tell me no."

I stared at him, my eyes wide, my hands shaking.

He inhaled slowly and then released it. "You understand that, correct? I will be a part of this child's life, whether you want me to or not. If that child is mine, I'm going to raise my child—not some other man."

He turned and walked to the door, which was still open. He paused as he started to walk out. "Acknowledge that you heard me, Riley."

I nodded slowly.

"Good. We will talk later. I have some thinking to do." With that, he stepped out of my house and closed the door with a hard thud.

The moment the door closed, my knees gave out, and I slumped to the floor, every muscle in my body quivering. What the hell did he mean about him raising the child and not another man?

CHAPTER SIXTEEN

ETHAN

*T*he week had been harsh. When I wasn't in class, I was trying to remain focused on my homework. If I didn't stay focused, thoughts drifted into my mind of my mother, and I couldn't allow myself to fall apart right now.

If I could just make it to Saturday, I could allow myself to grieve for a couple of days and then get back here and tackle my studies again.

Friday, I cut out of class an hour early to make my flight back to Millerstown, and of course, my flight was late arriving. By the time I got back to my house, it was after eleven. I was looking forward to cracking open a beer, reaching out to my sister, and then getting some sleep. I would need my rest tonight because tomorrow would take an emotional toll on all of us.

On my way home, I'd gotten a text from Henley. *Let me know when you're home.*

He didn't say anything else, and I wondered if something had happened. Maybe he was checking on me. I shot him back a message that I was home as soon as I walked in, and not five minutes later, there was a bang on my door.

Damn, he must have been right around the corner. I pulled it open, intent on inviting him in to join me for a beer. The look on his face immediately told me that something was up, but it was the fist to my cheekbone that landed that thought home.

I sputtered as I stepped backward, and he bum-rushed me up against the wall, his arm at my throat. "You son of a bitch!"

"What the hell is your problem?"

"You knocked up my sister!"

The world tilted as I stared at him. "What the fuck are you talking about, Lee?"

"Riley! She's pregnant, you son of a bitch, and every time she's tried to talk to you, you haven't given her a chance! No! Instead, you've been nasty as hell to her, and she runs from you crying!"

My blood had gone cold. "Henley, there is no way! How do you know this?"

He let go of my throat and put some distance between us. "She told me on Tuesday afternoon after she tried to tell you the *second* time. She tried to tell you before you left for training, but both times, you've gotten on her case, and she hasn't felt safe telling you."

"Felt safe? I would never do anything to hurt her."

"Yeah, well, that's not how she felt. Now it makes sense why she never left the house when she wasn't working, and why she was sick for weeks and lost weight."

"What do you mean she lost weight?"

"She had morning sickness, you moron! Couldn't eat at all for a few weeks."

I ran my hands over my head. Was it possible that he was telling the truth? I lifted my face to him. "On the off chance that you're going to hit me again, how do I know it's mine?"

Henley glared at me, and his lips twitched. "Because I know it is. You can ask her for those particulars. You need to fix this, Ethan!" He shoved his finger into my face. "You are not going to walk away from my sister and leave her pregnant and her baby fatherless."

"I would never do that," I hissed at him. "You know me better than that."

"Yeah, well, I thought you were a different kind of man. Had I known you'd made my sister cry the first time, I would have gotten on a plane and come down there to kick your ass!"

I hung my head. "I'll go talk to her."

"You better fix this, man. Or you're going to have more than just me on your ass. You're going to have three other brothers ready to tan your damn hide!"

He left as quickly as he had come, and I closed the door and stood there for a moment. Was Riley pregnant? Could it possibly be mine? Was that what was in her eyes on Tuesday morning? Had she come here to tell me, and I hadn't given her a chance because I'd been jealous that she'd known about my mother's illness and I hadn't?

I grabbed my keys off the side table and took off for her house. I didn't care if it was late; I needed to know the truth, and I needed to know it now!

On the way over to her house, my frustration and weariness swirled into a heated mixture of anger. She barely opened the door when I snapped at her. "Why didn't you tell me?"

Her eyes went wide, with both surprise and fear. "What are you talking about?"

"Don't play games, Riley. Why didn't you tell me you were pregnant?" I wasn't in the mood to beat around any bushes tonight.

"Did Henley tell you that?"

"What difference is it who told me? You should have, Riley! If it's even mine." I didn't mean to say that last part, but it came out regardless.

"Get out!"

So she could deny it more? Ha! No. "Not until you tell me the truth, Riley. Are you pregnant?"

She glared at me with that fiesty expression on her face that I had loved for so long. "I am."

My voice lowered slightly. "Is it mine?" Suddenly, I needed her to confirm that it was. I had to know if this was true.

Her flippant comment hit the wrong button, and I wanted to lose my mind. I couldn't deal with one more thing this week. Between flying back and forth from Georgia to PA, losing my mom, trying to stay in contact with my siblings and father, and now this. Fuck! I was ready to lose my shit completely!

"Oh, no, Riley. You are going to tell me the damn truth." I swallowed. "Unless you don't know if it's mine or not."

"It's your child, Ethan." I sighed internally. Riley was carrying my child. She was having my baby. How many times had I thought about that in the past and wished that it would happen?

Even though I knew she wouldn't lie to me about this, I had to ask. "How do I know it's mine?"

"Because I hadn't slept with anyone for about two months before we slept together, and I haven't been with anyone since."

"You expect me to believe that?" She was dating that Newman guy. There was no way she hadn't slept with him.

"You can believe whatever the hell you want!" she yelled back at me, but in her eyes, I saw it was the truth, and my anger began to subside.

"Why didn't you tell me, Ry?"

I listened to her speak and berated myself for being so frustrated both of those times. If I had just been calmer with her, I would have learned this sooner. How far along was she? I tried to count back, but my mind was a mess.

"Look, I don't want anything from you, Ethan. You don't even have to be part of this child's life if you don't want to."

She did not just say that! Did she seriously think I was going to allow her to raise our child with another man? That I wasn't going to be involved with my own child? Oh, hell, no! The words tumbled out of my mouth, and I barely knew what I was saying.

All I knew was that I needed to get out of the house and put some distance between us. I had a lot of thinking to do, but tonight was not the time to do it.

When I got home, I collapsed on the sofa with a beer in my hand and rested it against my swollen cheekbone. Until now, I hadn't paid much attention to it, but damn, Hen had clocked me one good. I deserved it.

As I thought back on tonight, along with the two times she had come to tell me, I realized how right she was. I hadn't given her a chance to talk. I sure hadn't made her feel comfortable enough to share that news with me, and tonight? Holy shit, I had acted like more of a Neanderthal than I ever had. Man, I needed to do some serious apologizing and figure out how to deal with this calmly.

Riley did not deserve my anger. She hadn't done this alone. It took two, which meant that it would continue to take two.

Saturday morning, I collected my suit and drove over to my father's. Candy and Carmen were there already, and I hugged them tightly before hanging my suit near the stairs.

I glanced around the living room, taking in the half dozen flower bouquets and two dozen cards on the mantel. I stood in front of them, letting my eyes drift over the words on the front of the cards. What did those words mean? What did I'm sorry mean? This last week, two dozen people had said I'm sorry for your loss, but what the fuck did that really mean? Only a few people had said it differently, and it was those people that I appreciate more than I could have asked for.

Those few had said that they had lost their mother or father, and they knew how hard it was. They had been devastated, and even a year or five later, it still hit them some days that they were gone. One guy said that every once in awhile, it was like someone punched him in the solar plexus, and he couldn't breathe for a moment. I understood that. I could relate to that. None of those people said they were sorry. They did say that with time, the pain would be less.

I stepped away from the cards and went back to the kitchen to help with breakfast. At eleven, we were all dressed and somber as the town car arrived. My father stared at it, shook his head, and then slowly approached it.

I could not imagine what was going through his mind. Coral and Cara sat on either side of him, and I sat beside Carmen, holding her hand.

At the funeral home, we were given time to view Mom alone before others joined us. My sisters walked my father forward, and I stumbled over my feet when I first saw her. This was the first I had seen her since she died—the first I had seen her since I left in June.

Coming up on her in the coffin was overwhelming, and I sobbed softly as I stared down at my sweet mother. Her silver hair was brushed neatly, her favorite dress on her.

We all cried and held each other, and then it was time for us to line up and accept condolences. Many times I had walked the line as someone paying respect to a grieving family member. I had never thought much about the people receiving them. Now everything was so much different.

The first ones through were the Youngs. The entire family came together, and with them, more tears were shed by us. I had yet to make eye contact with Riley, but she was coming my way. When she stopped in front of me, I took in her face, her bright but sad eyes, and I opened my arms to her. Riley fell into them, and the two of us stood like that for much longer than anyone else.

Her hand came to the back of my neck. "I'm so sorry, Ethan. I'm so sorry." She cried softly, and I wasn't sure if this was just about my mother or about everything else. Riley pulled back and cupped my cheek, wiping away a few tears that had run down, then she stepped forward and placed a single kiss on my cheek.

I wanted to pull her back into my arms and tuck her into my side. I wanted her to stay right there with me because at that moment, I needed her strength. I needed her to be here for me. I just needed her.

Instead, I shared a sad smile with her as she stepped on to my brother, and I accepted a hug from Patricia.

CHAPTER SEVENTEEN

RILEY

*E*ven though I had been exhausted last night, I had
barely slept. I kept hearing Ethan's words in my head,
saying that he would be involved in raising the child, not some
other man. What did he mean by that?

Was he saying that he wanted a voice in everything? Or did
he expect us to be in a relationship? I was so confused.

But that would all have to wait because we needed to get
through the day, and I would not cause him any undue stress
today. There would be plenty of time for that later.

Stepping away from him at the funeral was hard. I had
immediately wanted to wrap myself around him and protect
him from the pain and sadness of today, but I couldn't. I wasn't
even sure he would want me to. When I stepped away, I took a
seat two rows back and chatted quietly with Charlotte about
how I was physically feeling.

I would glance up periodically and find Ethan either focused
on the person in front of him or me. I wasn't sure if I was
calming him or making him angry again, and I was ready to
remove myself from the room, but I didn't.

As they got seated for the service, Ethan approached me and held out his hand. I didn't hesitate to take it, and he led me to the front row to sit with the family. Obviously, Ethan needed someone to lean on, and he had chosen me.

For years we had leaned on one another, and I didn't think much of it. Whatever he felt for me, whatever anger he harbored, we had a truce today.

I sat beside him, and he pulled my hand into his lap and held on to it with both hands. During the first prayer, I felt a teardrop land on my skin and roll between our hands. I squeezed his hand harder.

Our hands remained together through the service, and as the other guests were asked to step out so the family could pay their last respects, he had looked at me and said two words. "Stay, please."

I nodded and remained at his side, even when he went to the casket. He spoke softly, and I knew that no one could hear him. "I'm going to miss you so much, Momma. I wish you were going to be here to see your first grandchild. I wish I had at least gotten the chance to tell you."

I put my hand over Ethan's as it lay over his mother's. "She knew."

He turned to me. "What?"

"She knew. We talked about it."

He started to cry, and I did the only thing I could think of; I opened my arms and pulled him to me.

When he could speak again, he whispered against my ear, "I want to know everything that you said to her and everything that she said to you."

I nodded, rubbing my head against the side of his. It would be a sad conversation for us both, but I would share it with him. I had always planned to share it with him.

When we got outside, Ethan kissed my cheek and released me so that I could ride with my family to the cemetery.

Henley put his arm around me. "You okay?"

"Yeah, I'm okay."

"Was he an ass?"

I sighed. "Let's just say that we have a lot to talk about." I turned to him. "You didn't need to punch him."

He grinned. "Yeah, actually, I did. He did knock up my baby sister out of wedlock."

"What?" a deep voice behind me asked, and a hand landed on my shoulder. Henley and I glanced at each other quickly as he winced. Wesley stood behind us, his face stone-cold. "Tell me what I just heard was a joke."

"Wes, we'll talk about this later," I said to him and turned to walk away, but he grabbed my arm.

"No, is he serious? Are you pregnant, Ry?"

"Shh!" I hushed him, but it was evident by several other shocked faces around us that they had overheard him.

Tonya squealed. "Aunt Riley, you're having a baby?"

Brad pulled his daughter back but leaned forward. "Is this true?"

Oh, I wanted to throttle Henley! I was just about to snap at all of them when my mother put her arm around me and smiled. "Stop it, boys. Your sister is a big girl. We will discuss this at a more appropriate time. Get in your cars, and stop making a scene."

She hustled me toward their car, even though I had come with Roxy and Henley.

"You knew?" I whispered toward her.

She nodded as she glanced my way. "Of course, I have known. I've been waiting weeks for you to announce it so I could talk to you about it."

"Mom, why didn't you say anything?" I asked her as I climbed into the back seat of my dad's truck. He kept his face forward, and I could tell by the set of his jaw, he already knew too. Well, shit!

"Riley, I didn't want to invade your privacy."

"I'm sorry," I said softly as I picked at one of my nails, and she turned to look back at me.

"Don't apologize to me. I assume that Ethan knows now."

"Yeah, he found out last night."

She nodded. "Good. What did he say?"

"We didn't get much time to talk about it, and he was pretty upset at first."

My father glanced over his shoulder at me, and I held my hand up. "But he did say that he would be there every step of the way." My father gave a curt nod as if that was what he had wanted to hear.

Holy crap! Like we all needed this drama today!

"I'm sure you two will work it all out. We will talk about this later," my mother said, and I was glad we were putting the conversation to bed. As the procession started to leave the funeral home, I got a text message from Roxy.

Henley says he's sorry.

Oh, he better find a way to make it up to me.

A moment later, she responded. *He said free babysitting anytime.*

Well, that didn't seem like a bad trade. *Fine, but I'm still furious with him.*

The gravesite ceremony was quick and to the point, and before I knew it, we were resting roses on the casket and stepping away. Our family moved over to the side, and Ethan's family slowly trickled toward us. When Ethan joined us, he stood behind me, his hand on my lower back, and I leaned into him slightly.

My brothers all but glared daggers at him, but I wasn't sure he noticed as he put his mouth to my ear. "You are coming back to my parents' house, right?" He winced as he glanced at the casket. "It's always going to be my parents' house even if she's not there."

"Yes, I will be there. Henley, Coral, and I are cooking."

He nodded solemnly at me and then brushed a kiss over my cheek before he walked back to the town car they had come in.

"Is he going to marry you?" Wes asked as he blocked my view.

"No!" I hissed at him.

"Why not?"

"Look, Wes, I know all of you don't think that I can handle this, but I can. So please do me a favor and back off. Ethan has a lot going on right now, and the last thing he needs is you all ganging up on him."

"You damn well know that I can't *not* say something."

"You damn sure will keep your mouth shut! Today is not about me or what is happening. It's about them losing their mother. So stick a sock in it, big brother, and let it go. When I need a knight in shining armor, I'll let you know." I stalked around him and went back to my parents' truck as I rolled my eyes.

Henley, Coral, and I were busy heating things up and making sure the plates were out. I had tried to get Coral out of the kitchen, but she said she needed to be busy right now. I guess I could understand that.

Ethan came into the kitchen and stood watching us work. "What can I do to help?"

"Nothing," I replied with a kind smile.

"You can tell me what you're going to do with my sister."

"Wes!" I snapped at him as he reached Ethan. Henley rushed around the counter to push Wes back.

"Whoa, whoa, whoa. This is not the place, Wes," Henley said in a hushed voice.

Coral stared at them. "What's going on?"

"Hey, Wes." Ethan put his hands up in front of him. "No offense, but this is between Riley and me."

"Afraid not. Family is there for family. You know that."

"What the hell is going on?" Coral raised her voice, and just then, Brad stepped into the room, Carmen and Tonya behind him.

"Nothing," I tried to tell her.

Tonya came over to me. "Aunt Riley, when is the baby due?"

"You're pregnant?" Coral snapped, and Carmen gasped.

I picked up the dish I had in my hand and slammed it on the counter. I sure was glad that it didn't shatter, because that would have been my luck right then. However, I got the attention that I wanted.

"There is not one person in this room beside Ethan and me that have a right to talk about this. Yes, I am pregnant. Yes, he is the father. Now all of you butt the hell out until we have time to work things out."

I turned and stalked to the back door, shoving the squeaking thing open and rushing out. I heard Ethan's voice behind me, but not what was said.

I heard the door open and glanced back to yell at whoever was coming out, but I saw that it was Ethan. I resigned myself to having to discuss this with him whether I wanted to or not.

He approached slowly, stopping about three feet away. "How far along are you?"

"Nine weeks."

"When did you find out?"

"The day before you left for training. I was only four weeks then."

"You came over that night to tell me?"

I nodded and crossed my arms tightly over my chest. "Yes, and you told me that you had to put distance between us and you were moving on. I couldn't tell you. The words just wouldn't come out, not with how angry you were."

He shook his head and hung it for a minute. "I'm sorry."

"It's okay. I'm sorry about Henley hitting you."

He touched his cheek. "I deserved it."

"Why do you say that?"

"Because I was an ass to you. Before I left and you wouldn't admit that you loved me, I kind of lost it. I was jealous as hell of Newman—shit. I've been jealous of every single man you have been with for the last ten years, Riley."

"I'm sorry, Ethan. I'm sorry that I wasn't able to be what you wanted."

He stepped forward slightly. "The only thing that I wanted was for you to be with me. We were always good together. We've been friends forever. We know everything about one another."

"We are good friends," I replied, my stomach quivering as I tried to figure out where he was going with this conversation.

Ethan stepped closer, taking my face in his hands and lifting my chin up. He stared down at me. "Riley, I have been in love with you since I was sixteen years old. I would do anything for you, including be here with you every single step of the way. I don't know how you feel about me or about having this baby, but I need you to know that I will help you with anything. I will never leave you alone to deal with this—any of it."

I put my hands on his sides, needing to feel him. "Ethan, I know you love me. Right now, I am so confused and scared. I don't know how I feel about anything, except that I know that I don't want to do this alone. I want your help with this."

He smiled down at me, his blue eyes twinkling, and I realized how much I had missed him smiling at me like that. I raised up on my toes and pressed my lips to his. The kiss was tender, loving, and as he stepped back, he looked down at my belly.

"Are you really carrying my child, Riley?"

"Yes, Ethan, I am."

He grinned and pulled me into his arms, lifting me off the ground and staring me in the eye. "I'm gonna be a pretty damn good dad."

"That's what your mother said. She said that you would be a wonderful father."

He began to blink rapidly as he rested his forehead against mine. "Will you come over tonight so we can talk? I have a million questions, or I can come to you."

"Yeah, I think that it's time we talk."

CHAPTER EIGHTEEN

ETHAN

I knew that Riley and I weren't a couple, but if she hadn't been by my side during the service, I'm not sure I would have made it. The words the pastor said, the stories people shared, the tears on my father's face, all dug right down into the very depth of my soul, and it felt like knives were shredding it.

Her hand in mine, her thumb every once in a while brushing the skin, well, that kept me grounded. A few times, my mind drifted from the service, and I'd remember that Riley was carrying my child. Our baby was growing in her belly—not her baby, our baby!

Part of me wanted to stand up and shout for everyone to know, but we needed to talk before I did that. Riley and I had a lot to discuss, and I knew it wouldn't happen overnight.

As I said my final goodbyes to my mother, I wished that I could have shared the news with at least her. When Riley said she had, I sobbed into her hair. Knowing that my mother knew the secret before even I did somehow felt right. I could not wait to hear the conversation that they shared.

I managed to get through the graveside service, and then we

were heading back to the house. The day was an emotional whirlwind, and I was ready to get rid of everyone and drink myself into oblivion.

Actually, that wasn't what I wanted. What I wanted to do was sit down with Riley and talk. I was heading into the kitchen to see if I could speak to her or at least help when Wes came at me. It got a little wild for a few minutes, and then Riley, being Riley, slammed a dish down on the counter and got everyone's attention.

Like everyone else in the room, I was a little shocked at her blurting it all out, but hey, we were talking about Riley here.

"Ethan, did you know about this?" Coral asked as she wiped her hands on a towel.

I put my hands up. "I think Riley said it very well. Once we get a chance to talk, we will fill you all in." I started to turn away and then got in Wes's face. "And as for my intentions with your sister, I would never leave her high and dry. You know how I feel about her."

I stalked away and found her walking circles in the backyard.

As I approached her, I looked her over. She didn't look pregnant, and I still hadn't figured out how far along she was. "How far along are you?"

"Nine weeks."

We talked for a few moments, and I felt like an ass. I really had treated her like shit. I had been doing that to protect myself, but in doing that, I had hurt her. I never wanted to hurt Riley. I had been a jealous asshole and had lashed out. I was better than that.

"I'm sorry, Ethan. I'm sorry that I wasn't able to be what you wanted."

"The only thing that I wanted was for you to be with me. We were always good together. We've been friends forever. We know everything about one another."

"We are good friends."

I needed to touch her. I had held back long enough, and I couldn't do it any longer. "Riley, I have been in love with you since I was sixteen years old. I would do anything for you, including be here with you every single step of the way. I don't know how you feel about me or about having this baby, but I need you to know that I will help you with anything. I will never leave you alone to deal with this—any of it."

"Ethan, I know you love me. Right now, I am so confused and scared. I don't know how I feel about anything, except that I know that I don't want to do this alone. I want your help with this."

I knew she didn't love me, but maybe she would come to do so. Perhaps she already did but was afraid of loving someone. I vowed then that I would wait; I would show her that she needed me, that she loved me more than just as a friend.

"Are you really carrying my child, Riley?"

"Yes, Ethan, I am."

Finally, excitement exploded through me, and I lifted her in the air and twirled her around. "I'm gonna be a pretty damn good dad."

"That's what your mother said. She said that you would be a wonderful father."

I put her feet down and closed my eyes as her words settled over me. "Will you come over tonight so we can talk? I have a million questions, or I can come to you."

"Yeah, I think that it's time we talk."

Since Riley didn't have a car here, I told her I would take her home. The two of us walked back into the house, arm in arm. After a few glares from her brothers, I kissed her forehead and left the room. Riley was right; it was our business, and after we figured things out, we would let them know.

By the time the last friend left, every single one of us was exhausted. In fact, Riley was up in my room napping, and I slipped into the room without disturbing her. She was curled on her side, her hands tucked under her chin. I lifted a curl and wrapped it around my finger, and she shifted.

She opened her eyes after I squatted down. "Hey, sleepyhead."

"What time is it?"

"Almost seven."

"Seven?" She rolled to her back and stretched, and my gaze went to her belly. "Sorry, I didn't mean to sleep that long."

"It's okay, but why don't you get up, and I'll take you home."

I helped her get up, and after she stood, she swooned slightly, grabbing my arm. "Sorry, stood too fast."

"Are you okay? Do you need anything? Do you want to lie down again?"

Riley laughed and slapped her hand over my mouth. "I'm fine. I stood up too fast."

She was right. I was overreacting, but how could I not now that I knew she was pregnant? She was only nine weeks, which meant she had another thirty-one weeks to go. Another thirty-one weeks where I was going to be worried sick about her.

I paused halfway down the stairs as I remembered that I was flying back to Georgia tomorrow night, and I would be there for another seven weeks. How the hell would I be able to watch over her from there? How far along was she going to be when I returned, sixteen weeks? What was I missing during the next seven weeks?

I forced myself down the stairs and followed Riley into the living room to say goodbye to my sisters and father. My father hugged her tightly, spoke softly to her for a moment, and then shook my hand.

"You do right by that young lady."

"Yes, sir."

He told me to make sure I came to see him the next day before I left, and I promised him I would.

At Riley's, I followed her into the house and locked the door behind me. I had no intentions of leaving her side tonight. I'd sleep on the couch, I didn't care, but I was staying with her until I had to go.

Riley kicked off her shoes and said that she was going to change into more comfortable clothes. She was upstairs for a few minutes before she returned, carrying a pair of my lounge pants and a t-shirt in her hands. "Here, I figured you were tired of the suit."

"When did you steal these?"

She shrugged. "Probably the last time I slept over there and didn't feel like putting my dress clothes back on from the night before."

I hesitated outside the bathroom door. "Riley, don't get angry with me for asking, but have you been drinking since you found out?"

She lifted her face and stared at me. "Not one drop since I found out, and maybe one or two beers before that."

I nodded and stepped into the bathroom to change. I folded my suit and put it on one of the chairs before I came to sit on the couch beside her. In her hands was a big glass of water.

"What did you want to talk about?" she asked, glancing at me nervously.

"I want to hear everything about the baby. I want to know how you feel, what you thought when you first found out. Hell, Riley, I want to know where you bought the test."

She chuckled. "Well, I was pretty sick at first, and I couldn't even think of eating meat or drinking coffee."

"Oh, that would be rough for you."

"Yes, it was. That's how I lost about six pounds. I thought I had a stomach bug, but one night I was out and tried to eat a slice of pizza and rushed to the bathroom. The waitress said something about how she had done that same thing when she

141

was pregnant. I knew as soon as she mentioned it. It was like everything just made sense."

She took a deep breath and sipped her water before she continued. "So after Joe dropped me off that night—"

"Joe? You're still seeing him?"

"I am."

I frowned. "Riley, are you sure this baby is mine?"

She pursed her lips. "Unless he can get me pregnant by kissing me, there is no way it is his. I have never slept with him, and if you ask me that question one more time, I am going to smack you upside the head, Ethan Winston."

I chuckled. "Okay, I believe you."

"I've never lied to you, Ethan. I won't ever lie to you."

Oh, the urge to ask her if she loved me was on the tip of my tongue, but I didn't want to hear her say no.

"So continue with your story."

"After he brought me home, I went out to buy a test. It was positive, and I knew I needed to tell you, but you weren't all that receptive to seeing me."

I winced. "Riley, I apologized. I'm sorry. I was trying to let you go and protect myself. I was an ass, but I was doing what I thought was right."

"I know you were, and I'm sorry that I blew that up. What is your girlfriend going to say about this?"

"Sam is not my girlfriend."

She spiked a brow. "Oh really? I saw her kissing you on the porch."

I sighed. "Riley, I was trying to move on. Sam and I had an arrangement. She's in my class. She knows all about you, and she's still in love with her ex-husband. She lives in New York."

"It's just sex between you two?"

"It *was* just sex between us."

Riley frowned. "What's that supposed to mean?"

I reached over the couch and gently pulled her hand toward

me. I took the glass out of her hand and set it on the table. Then I got as close to her as I could. "Whatever it was that I was doing with Sam is over. Just like I hope that whatever you were doing with Joe is over. Riley, I know you don't love me, but can you give me a chance to show you that I can give you a good life? That I can give our baby a good life?"

"Ethan, what are you asking?"

"I'm asking you to give us, you and me, a chance. I'm not asking you to marry me, Riley, so don't freak out, but I'm asking you to consider taking a chance on us. Can we see if we can build a relationship that will help us create a solid foundation for our child?"

Her eyes bounced back and forth between mine. "I don't know, Ethan. I won't lie to you and tell you that I haven't secretly dreamed that you would drop down on one knee and propose, but I can't say that I want to commit to you as someone I am in a relationship with either."

I grinned. "You actually thought about me proposing?"

"Yeah, in a perfect world, we'd be head over heels in love, and we'd get married, raise a family, and live happily ever after, but this isn't one of Daniella's novels. This is real life. I'm not sure I'm capable of that. You know me."

I put my finger over her lips. "I do know you, Riley, and I know that if you gave it a chance—a real chance—then you'd see I am right." I lifted her chin with my knuckle. "Just give it a chance, Riley. Can you do that for me? For our baby?"

She sighed. "I can try."

I leaned forward and pressed my lips to hers, then shifted my face slightly to the side as I kissed her again. Another kiss and Riley was starting to lean toward me. Her lips parted, and I wasted no time slipping my tongue into her mouth. She whimpered and, a split second later, began to climb over my lap to straddle me.

CHAPTER NINETEEN

RILEY

$\mathcal{M}$y pregnancy hormones went from zero to a hundred in a matter of one tongue swipe. Suddenly, I needed to be touched, held, loved! It had been nine weeks since I'd wanted this.

Well, that wasn't true; there were times when I'd been with Joe, and we'd been making out, and I'd wanted a release, but it wasn't Joe's body that I had craved.

I had craved Ethan's.

I was on his lap, holding his face between my hands as I kissed him as if the existence of my very soul was at stake. Ethan's hand skimmed up my spine to my head, where he tugged my hair out of the messy bun that I'd put it up in. His hands ran through my long locks before he shifted them back down to lift my shirt off. I pulled back enough to get it over my head, and then I was right back there against him, whimpering as his hands cupped my swollen breasts. He groaned—and then there was a knock at the door.

I pulled back from Ethan, dazed as we stared at one another. Another knock sounded, and I grabbed my shirt off the couch where Ethan had dropped it and held my finger up to him as I rushed to the door. Whoever was outside was going to be taking a walk.

I yanked open the door and froze. "Joe! What are you doing here?"

"Hi, I was checking on you, sweetheart. I know today was a hard day." He started to step forward and then paused, his eyes shifting to my shirt. He stepped back. "Did I interrupt something?"

"No, I'm just tired."

The door that I was holding tightly yanked back, and I stumbled backward into Ethan as he asked, "Who is it, *sweetheart?*"

Ethan stepped to my side and glared at Joe, and I did a double take when I saw he'd taken his shirt off, and damn if his hard-on wasn't pointing proudly right at Joe.

Joe's eyes shifted, and his jaw tensed. "Ethan, I didn't know you were here. I'm sorry to hear about your mother. I lost mine a few years ago. I know how hard it is."

Ethan actually deflated slightly. "Thanks."

Joe turned back to me. "Since you two seem busy, I'll just go." He started to turn, and I stepped forward and grabbed his arm.

"Joe, I'm sorry, this isn't what it seems like."

He looked past me, staring at Ethan for a moment, and then smiling at me. "I think it might be, but I get it. Good night, Riley."

"Joe, wait! Can you meet me for coffee tomorrow? I will explain what is going on. You deserve an explanation." I gnawed on my bottom lip as I pleaded with my eyes.

"Okay, I should be available around eight. I have to get the kids by ten."

"Okay, I'll text you in the morning."

He didn't say anything else as he turned and walked away. I watched him get into his car, and then after he pulled out of my driveway, I spun on Ethan.

"That was not very nice!" I hissed at him as I pushed him back into the house.

"What?"

"Don't you what me, Ethan! That was rude. You didn't need to do that and upset Joe."

"Yeah, well, he should be upset. You haven't told him that you're carrying another man's child."

I pursed my lips and walked around him. "You can leave now."

He laughed. "I'm not going anywhere tonight, Riley."

I started cackling as I dug inside the fridge. "I'm sorry, did you just say you weren't going anywhere? I'm pretty sure I heard you wrong because you aren't invited to stay."

I closed the fridge and saw him leaning against the wall beside it. "And I already decided that I'm staying tonight. We aren't done talking."

"Yes, we are."

"No, we aren't, Riley."

I poured a glass of milk and then stared at him. "Ethan, what else is there to talk about right now? I told you that I would give this a chance."

"Are you going to break it off with Joe tomorrow?"

"I'm pretty sure we are broken up, thanks to your pointed display at the door, but yes, I will tell him it's over." I lifted the glass and popped a hip against the counter as I stared at him. "You going to end it with your school friend?"

"It's over."

"Does she know that?"

"No, but she will as soon as I get back. Riley, she knows how I feel about you. She knows that I was trying to get over you. I don't think that she will be surprised when I tell her we got back together."

"Wait, I didn't say we were together, Ethan. I said I'd give it a chance. That does not mean that we are a couple."

His facial features darkened. "Riley, do not date anyone while you are carrying my child. Don't do that to me."

"That's kind of selfish of you to say. You can go around having sex with anyone you want, but I have to be celibate while I'm pregnant?"

"I didn't say that. Look, I won't sleep with anyone if you promise you won't."

"Until the baby is born."

A muscle ticked in his cheek. "Until the baby is born."

I huffed. "Fine." I drank my milk, rinsed out my glass, and then walked past him. "I'm going to bed. If you aren't going home, you are sleeping on the couch." I heard him chuckle as I hit the stairs.

I was upstairs for an hour before my stomach growled and I was suddenly craving chocolate sauce. I didn't want the ice cream to go with it, just chocolate sauce. I could imagine tipping my head back and squirting it right into my mouth, or better yet, squirting it over Ethan's chest and licking it off.

I pulled the pillow over my head. Ever since I came up here, I'd been waiting for him to knock on my door, or more like barge right in, but he hadn't. A few minutes ago, I got up to use the bathroom and peered outside to see his truck still in front of my house.

What was he doing down there? Was he thinking about me? Was he watching television? Was he wishing he was up here in my bed having sex? Oh, my god! I wished he was. How was I going to make it another seven months without sex?

The thought of chocolate sauce filled my mind again. Maybe I could slip into the kitchen without him noticing and get the bottle in the fridge. Maybe he would be asleep or engrossed in a movie.

I tiptoed down the stairs, listening carefully and hearing the television on in the living room. I hugged the wall as I went down the hallway and peered into the living room to find him on the couch, his feet kicked out on the coffee table. Damn!

I glanced at the kitchen. The chocolate sauce was screaming for me. I started to turn back around, but then I growled to myself and walked as quietly as possible into the kitchen.

I got down on my hands and knees behind the counter so he wouldn't see me and crawled to the fridge. If I stayed on my knees and just slipped my hand into the fridge, I could grab the chocolate sauce before he would see the light on, right?

At the fridge, I got up on my knees and peered toward the living room, but I couldn't see the couch. Coast was clear. I cracked open the fridge just enough to get my hand inside and tried to move it to where the chocolate sauce should be. I had to open it a bit more, but finally, I located the bottle. I took it out as quietly as I could, bringing it right to my mouth and squirting some inside.

"What are you doing?"

I jumped, and chocolate sauce sprayed over my face as I spun on my knees. He was standing two feet behind me, his arms crossed, his chest still bare, and on my knees, oh, my god, he was at the right height. I wiped the sauce off my face, thinking about drizzling it over his hard-on. I got dizzy at the thought and licked my lips.

"I wanted chocolate sauce," I said softly. I glanced at Ethan's face, but his beautiful eyes couldn't hold my attention when it was his abs that were screaming for me. They wanted to be coated in sweet sauce and licked off.

"Riley, whatever you are thinking about, stop."

I smiled. "Why? Because we aren't having sex with anyone while I am pregnant. I didn't know that included each other. I thought it was just other people."

I walked on my knees toward him, put the chocolate sauce bottle tip in my mouth again, and sucked a little bit of it out.

That erection that had deflated was back, and it was only inches away from me and chocolate heaven.

I paused when I was within reach and stared up at him. He always did love it when I was on my knees. Even in my alcoholic haze, I knew he loved me there. I leaned forward, rubbing my cheek on the outline of his erection. He hissed but otherwise didn't move.

I set the bottle down and shimmied his pants off his hips, my sex clenching as his came into view. I retrieved the bottle of chocolate and peered up at him. His eyes were wide, his lips parted.

I drizzled a little of the chocolate over his shaft and up to his head, then used my finger to smear it a little bit. He sucked in a sharp breath and his hands fisted at his sides. I licked my lips again as I stared up at him, and then I leaned forward, watching him as I flicked my tongue over his head.

His eyes enlarged, and he stared at my tongue as it trailed over the tender shaft. I pulled him deep into my mouth, and his head fell back on a groan. "Fuck!"

Another few deep sucks and his hands came to my face as he stared down at me and pumped his hips slightly. I leaned back so I could get more chocolate, and Ethan bent down and pulled me to my feet. His mouth crashed against mine, and then he pulled my hair back. My neck was open to him as his mouth moved to right under my ear.

Ethan lifted me higher into his arms, and my feet came off the floor. I wrapped my legs around him, clinging to him as he started to walk us out of the room. He paused and looked at me. "Where is the chocolate?"

I showed him my hand, the bottle still tightly grasped. He grinned and took us down the hallway and up the stairs. He dropped me on the bed, and without any preamble, yanked my pants off my legs before he dropped to his knees. "Give me the chocolate."

I passed it to him and gasped as he drizzled the chocolate over my lower abdomen, then lower still. The cold syrup was a shock to my hot lady parts, and he set the bottle aside as he began to lick the sauce away.

He worked his way over my stomach, pausing to kiss it gently right in the center as he looked up at me. Then while keeping his eyes locked on mine, he licked me right up the center, and my body tensed. It was not going to take me much to hit the top. "Please!" I begged him, and he answered with a grunt as he put his mouth to me and sucked.

I hit the top not once, but twice, and then Ethan was over me and about to enter. "Wait! You're not wearing protection."

He laughed. "I don't think I can get you any more pregnant than you are, Riley."

"No, you always wore a condom with me."

He thought for a second. "I didn't the last time we were together."

I blinked rapidly. "What? Why not?"

"Because you didn't give me a chance to put one on. You told me to forget it."

Oh, Jesus, had I said that?

"I figured since you were on the pill, it would be no big deal," he said, then studied me. "You were on the pill, right?"

I slowly shook my head. "No, I was coming off for a month because I was going to try a different form of birth control."

He laughed as he touched my face. "And that, dear Riley, is how you got knocked up."

"Shit!" I said. "I'm sorry, it's all my fault."

"Ry, don't worry about it. What happened, happened."

Suddenly, a tendril of fear began to slither through my gut. "Ethan, would you think I was strange if I said I was scared?"

His face softened, and he pressed a kiss to both of my cheeks before he rolled off of me. "Baby, I would not think you strange. I'm pretty sure that's a natural reaction for any parent."

My hand fluttered to my lower stomach, and Ethan brushed my hand aside and put his there. "And for the record, I'm scared too, but you and I are going to do this."

I shifted away from him for a moment and grabbed my cellphone off the nightstand.

"What are you doing?"

"Give me a second."

I brought up a video from the doctor's office and turned it toward Ethan before I hit play. His eyes went wide as he stared at the tiny fetus on the ultrasound. The steady fast thumping captured on the audio.

He blinked, and I saw tears in his eyes. "That's the baby?"

I nodded.

He watched it and then watched it again before he leaned down and kissed my stomach. "You don't know me yet, but I love you, little one."

CHAPTER TWENTY

ETHAN

f course, I heard her trying to sneak into the kitchen. I'd been waiting for her to do something like that for an hour. What I didn't expect was for her to start drinking the chocolate right from the bottle. And I sure as hell never expected her to come to me on her knees and put it on my throbbing dick.

Her sucking the chocolate sauce off was one of the most beautiful and erotic things I had ever seen. As I got to my knees between her legs, I felt as if I'd come home. Emotions swamped me as I carried her over, and I knew that I would never be happy again with any other woman.

Riley was my future. I just needed her to see that.

When Riley showed me the video, I was in awe. The baby was just this tiny little blob, but it was moving, and this little spot was flashing, along with this *whoosh-whoosh-whoosh* sound that I knew was the heart. That was my baby, mine and Riley's.

I leaned over her stomach. "You don't know me yet, but I love you, little one." I kissed her belly softly as a tear dropped to her skin and then another tear. I tried to stop, but suddenly, I remembered that my mother would never get to see this baby. Never get to see any of her grandchildren, and I began to sob.

"Ethan." Riley pulled me up so that she could curl herself around me and held me as I cried. One memory after another came forward of my mother, and I continued to cry, sometimes so hard that I thought I would explode. All the while, Riley held me, soothing me with soft kisses on my brow and strong arms around me.

I didn't know how long I cried, but once I stopped, she handed me several tissues and let me clean myself up. She excused herself to the bathroom, and when she came back, she slipped her pajama pants back on and climbed in bed.

I used her bathroom, and when I came back, she was lying on her side, the opposite side of the bed turned down. I slid in beside her and opened my arms to her. She came to me, resting her head on my shoulder. "I'm sorry for that."

"Ethan, don't apologize. You're allowed to mourn."

"It was like it just hit me. I mean, I've cried a few times, but I couldn't hold it back. The thought of my mom never seeing her grandchild broke my heart."

She lifted her face off my chest. "She saw that video."

"She did?"

"Yeah." She nodded and lay back down. "She saw it."

"What did my mom say?"

"Well, she told me that you would be a wonderful father and that I should give you a chance. You know, she's the reason I decided to keep the baby."

"Wait." I felt my entire body stiffen. "You were going to get rid of it?"

Riley sighed. "At first, it was an option." She rested her chin on her hand on my chest. "I didn't want to do that, but I was scared. I wasn't sure I could have a child. I wasn't sure I even wanted one."

"How did my mother convince you?"

"She got sick."

"What?"

"I was on my way to see my doctor and get it confirmed. Plus, figure out my options, but I was a little early and sitting outside trying to gather the courage to go inside. I saw your parents coming out of the oncologist. They both looked devastated, and I figured out pretty quickly that whatever news they had learned wasn't good, and it probably had to do with your mom. I knew right then that I couldn't do anything *but* have this child."

The thought of her getting rid of our baby without me knowing made me cold inside. "Yeah, well, if you start considering that again, you better call me."

Riley chuckled. "Ethan, both our families know about this now. There is no way I could not have the baby."

I grinned. "True."

Riley sighed and then laid her head back on my chest as I ran my fingers over her shoulder and down her arm.

"What do you want? A boy or a girl?"

She shrugged. "I don't know, a boy would probably be easier. My luck, I'd have a really girlie girl, and I'd lose my mind."

I burst out a laugh. "But, man, it would be awesome to have a little mini you running around."

She snickered. "You say that now, Ethan. What about you?"

"I want one of each, so twins."

Her head popped off my chest. "Bite your tongue, and you just saw with your own eyes that it's only one."

"Okay, so after we have one, we'll just have to try again."

She rolled her eyes and exhaled in disgust. "One is all I am having with you."

"Just one? You mean in a few years, you won't consider having another one?"

She shrugged. "Maybe, but who knows if we will still be talking to one another."

I rolled her to her back before she knew what was happening. "Riley Young, you are stuck with me forever. You might not believe that, but you are."

"You think so, huh?"

I slipped my leg between hers. "I don't think so, I know so." I started kissing her neck as my hand slipped down to cup her breast. I loved that they were larger now and overflowed from my hand. "No other man makes you feel the way I do."

I pulled her shirt out of the way and suckled her breast. Even her nipples were a little larger, and my dick throbbed. I moved to her other one, then pressed them together, going back and forth between the two nipples as she watched.

She gasped and closed her eyes, her mouth parting as her breathing sped up. I slipped my hand into her pants, fingering her slick slit as she pressed against me.

I removed her pants, then mine as she removed her shirt, and I returned my mouth to her breast as I loved her with my fingers. When I couldn't take it anymore, and I knew she was close, I shifted over her and stared down at her as I entered.

She whimpered as she clung to my shoulders, and the two of us moved as one, kissing and touching until I felt my release building. I stared down into her face, and she would never admit it, but I saw love there. One day she would admit it to everyone.

We shattered together, and I found myself spent as I came down—both physically and emotionally spent. I rolled us to our sides and held her tightly as I immediately began to drift off to sleep. The love of my life and my child tucked close to me for safekeeping.

WHEN I WOKE UP SUNDAY, I found myself alone in bed and checked my watch to see it was already seven-thirty. Damn! I pulled on my pants and searched for Riley. There was a note on the table.

Ethan, sorry, had to go take care of the horses. I'll talk to you later. If I don't see you before you go, have a safe trip back to Georgia. Ry

I sighed and dropped the note. She was going to hide from me today, but there wasn't much I could do. Instead, I thought it over for a few minutes while I got dressed in my slacks and shirt from the day before, and then I sat down and wrote her a note.

Riley, I hope your breakup with Joe went smoothly. I have a flight early afternoon, so I probably won't see you. I will call you when I get back to my room tonight. Expect a phone call from me every night so I can check in with you and our baby. I want to know everything. I love you more than you know. Please be careful. Ethan

I left it on the table and let myself out. It was almost eight, so Riley would be someplace meeting Joe. I wished that I knew where so I could go watch, but I needed to see my father before I left.

I went back to my place, showered, and packed my things up before I went over to hang out there until I was ready to leave. My father was taking me to the airport today, and I was glad that we had a little bit of time to ourselves before I had to leave again.

"Dad, if you need anything, you let me know."

"Ethan, I know that, but I also have five other kids who can help me."

"Yeah, but the girls can't fix things around the house. Shit, Evan can't do that either."

"No, but I do know how to call a repairman, and I have David Young on speed dial."

I chuckled. "Yeah, I guess you do."

"Speaking of David, you and Riley get a chance to talk?"

"Yeah, Dad, we did. We talked for a while last night."

"And did you guys get things sorted out?"

"We are starting to. It's going to be hard with me in class for another several weeks; maybe I can get back for a weekend, but I'm not sure. Training gets more intense now, and I need to focus."

"Ethan, son, you focus on your job. Riley has a lot of people here who will be watching out for her."

"I just don't want her to do anything stupid."

"What? Like fall in love with another man? Or start drinking again?"

"No—well, yeah."

My father smirked. "Riley is a spitfire, she always has been, but she's not reckless. I think she realized that she was drinking a little bit too much, and the baby came at the perfect time to help her get through that. As for another man, she loves you."

"You know, sometimes I think that she does. Like I see it in her eyes, but then other times I feel like I'm making it up." I hesitated. "How did you know that Mom loved you?"

He smiled slowly as if a fond memory was coming to his mind. "I felt it in her touch, in the way she looked for me when we were in a crowd. Her eyes sparkled at me, but not at any other man, even if she was flirting with them, but it was her words that told me the most."

"Because she said she loved you?"

He shook his head. "No, because she trusted me enough to tell me everything. The good, the bad—everything. She told me her secrets, her fears, and because of that, I knew she loved me because you can't love someone fully if you can't trust them."

"Good point, Dad."

"I have a couple of those," he jested.

When he dropped me off, I hugged him tightly, and then the two of us looked at one another long and hard. I felt like a part of me was trying to memorize this moment in case he died while I was gone.

"Son." He put his hand around the back of my neck and stared at me hard. "I'm gonna be here when you get home."

Damn, how did the man know what I'd been thinking? "I know you will, Dad. I love you."

"And I love you. We will keep an eye on Riley for you. Don't you worry about her."

"Thanks, Dad." I gathered my bag and then disappeared into the terminal.

I was just sitting down at the gate when my phone vibrated with a text. I took it out and saw it was Riley. *Hope your flight was okay.*

I typed her back. *Haven't gotten on it yet, but thanks. How did it go with your breakup?*

Would you believe he broke up with me before I could do it to him?

Not surprised. You did have a half-naked man in your house last night, and your hair did look a little sex wild.

That's not funny, Ethan. A moment later, there was another message. *But seriously, he had come over to see me last night to break up with me. He said that he met someone else.*

Hallelujah! *Aw, darn,* I typed to her.

I know you are utterly heartbroken.

I truly am. I wanted to tell her that I loved her, but I didn't. Instead, I typed, *Tell my little one I love it. I'll talk to you tonight.*

Bye, Ethan. Your little one loves you back.

I stared at that message until my screen went blank. Yes, I was happy that she had told me that, but how I wish it had said *we* love you back.

CHAPTER TWENTY-ONE

RILEY

I stared at him sleeping, feeling things that I wasn't sure I wanted to feel. I crept from the bed and gathered clothes before I went to the guest bathroom and took a quick shower. I needed to feed the horses and then meet Joe for coffee.

Man, I hated how things went down with him last night, and I knew I had to be honest with him. I checked in with him as I left the house, and we decided on a diner on the edge of town rather than Coral's Coffee Café. The last thing I needed was her asking how the baby was as we placed our orders.

I was there a few minutes early, and I opted for tea instead of coffee. My stomach was feeling a little iffy, probably from the stress of what I was about to do. As I sat there waiting, I thought about the night before.

I'd never seen Ethan so vulnerable, and I would be stupid not to realize that he'd felt safe enough with me to let himself break to pieces. I didn't know many men who would do that. When Brad's wife died, I saw him cry a few times, but not break down in heart-shattering sobs. I could not imagine.

Ethan had made love to me last night, and again, I couldn't

deny that it was just that. It had *not* been sex. Maybe it had started as sex downstairs with the chocolate, but after bearing his broken heart, it had been more—way more. I had felt it in him, felt it in myself, and I wondered if he had noticed a difference with me.

It wasn't like I could ask him, but I hoped that maybe he knew I cared a little more than he initially thought. Was it love? Maybe.

Joe slipped into the seat across from me. "Morning, Riley. How was your night?"

I frowned. "Joe, I am very sorry about that."

He held his hand up. "Riley, don't apologize." He sighed. "I knew when I first saw you two together that I should never have gotten between you. You guys have a history together, and it's obvious that you both love one another."

I opened my mouth to deny it, and he put his palm up. "Save it, Riley. You can deny it all you want. Even when you were angry with him, I saw the way you looked at him."

"Joe, I'm sorry. I—" I blew out a frustrated breath. "I'm pregnant."

He leaned back slightly. "How long have you known that?"

"Um, since the night we went to the movies."

The waitress arrived at our table, and he turned his coffee mug over. "Just coffee."

After she left, he stared at me. "Is that why you didn't want to do anything else with the kids or sleep with me?"

I leaned forward. "Yes, that is exactly why. I was so confused and not sure what the hell I was going to do. I really liked you, but at the same time, I didn't know what you would say. I also didn't want to get the kids more involved if things weren't going to work for us." I winced. "And I didn't want to sleep with another man when I knew I was carrying someone else's baby."

He stirred cream in his cup as he contemplated what I'd said. After taking a sip, he nodded. "I appreciate that. Both of those, actually. I'm not sure how I would have felt if I found out you were pregnant by another man. Maybe if I had known he wasn't in the picture, it would have been different, but with Ethan—" He laughed. "He is a little territorial when it comes to you, Riley. When did you tell him?"

"He learned Friday night."

He nodded. "Well, I wish you two well. Are you guys going to try and work things out?"

"To be honest, Joe, I have no clue."

He reached over the table. "I think if you put your energy into it and stop trying to deny it, you two could have a great relationship."

"I don't know."

"He loves you, Riley. Only a blind fool wouldn't know that."

"I know he does."

"Do you love him?"

"The question isn't if I love him, I do, but it's if I love him enough and in the right way." I stopped. "Wait, is this weird to talk about?"

He chuckled and leaned forward. "Actually, I have a little confession to make."

"What's that?"

"I went out on another date the other night, and I was coming by last night to let you know that I wanted to keep seeing this other woman."

"You were coming over to break up with me?" I asked, surprised.

He nodded, looking slightly guilty. I grabbed his hands. "That's great, Joe!"

He chuckled and squeezed my hands before we both let go. "I think you and I will make much better friends and allies."

"Allies?"

He grimaced and then grinned. "Yeah, I kind of went out on a date with Carmen."

My jaw dropped. "Carmen Winston?"

"Yep."

I started laughing. "Are you serious? Oh, Ethan is going to love that!"

"Look, don't say anything to him yet. She didn't want it getting back to her family yet. She wanted to make sure things were good with us. She doesn't want to add stress to the family."

"Oh, I get it." I pretend to lock my lips shut and leaned forward, speaking softly. "So, it was a good date?" He grinned, and his cheeks started to turn pink. "Oh my god! You slept with Carmen!"

He hushed me, and I slapped a hand over my mouth and glanced around to see who might be watching. Other than an old couple two booths down, no one seemed to be paying us any attention.

"Yeah, so one thing led to another."

"Joe, that's great! I'm really happy for you. I hope that things work out for you two. I love Carmen. She's fantastic, but how did you two hook up?" I put my hand up. "Wait, she isn't counseling Chip, is she?"

"No, actually, I met her at the picnic you brought me to and then ran into her twice getting coffee before work. She asked how Chip was because I'd mentioned him before, and we got to talking. I ended up asking her out."

"Didn't she know that we were seeing each other?"

"She also knows that it would never have worked between us because of her brother."

"Oh, right." I nodded. "Well, that's great, Joe."

The two of us talked for a while and ended up ordering breakfast before he had to get to work. I drove over to my parents, knowing that I needed to face the music with them.

Luckily, only they were there, and I didn't have to deal with my siblings. When I walked in, I found my parents sitting at the table, looking at a photo album. I kissed them both on the top of the head. "What are you looking at?"

"Oh, just a few baby pictures," my mother said, and I wondered if they'd had that book sitting at the table ready for me to walk in.

I went to dig around in the fridge, not that I wanted anything to eat, but because I wasn't sure how to start this conversation.

"So what did you and Ethan finally decide?" my mother asked.

"Um, I'm not sure we've made any decisions, other than to see how things go."

"You mean between you and him, not with the baby, right?"

"We are having the baby, Mom, don't worry."

She grinned. "Oh, I wasn't, Riley."

"Then why did you ask?"

"You never know with you, Riley." She waved a hand at me. "What did you two talk about?"

I sank into a seat across the table from them, and my dad went to refill his coffee. "Ethan wants us to see if we can work things out."

"You mean, as in be a couple?"

"Yeah, I guess."

"You guess?" She laughed. "Riley, when are you going to wake up and see how much you care about him."

"Mom, stop. I do care about him, but I don't know if I feel enough to base a relationship off of—or get married for. I don't want to jump into something. I have a lot to think about, and Ethan has weeks more of class to focus on. When he gets back, we'll figure something out, but I told him I would try."

"Well, that's the best that you can do."

"When did you know that you were with child?" my father asked as he took a seat.

"About five weeks ago."

"And you just told Ethan about it this weekend?"

"Actually, I didn't tell him. Henley did."

"So your brother knew before Ethan? That doesn't seem right."

"Hen heard something Roxy said and wouldn't let it go until I told him. I had no idea he was going to hit Ethan."

"Your brother is protective. I'm sure Ethan could understand him being upset," my mother said.

"Yes, he never said anything about it to me."

"Well, I'm glad it's out now, and you are taking care of yourself."

"I am, Mom. I eat as well as I can, take my vitamins. I'm doing my yoga, and I haven't had a drink since I found out."

"Good. When will Ethan be back?"

"I don't know, really. Probably seven, eight weeks. We didn't talk about it."

"What are you going to do about Joe?"

"Oh, we broke up. He's already seeing someone else."

"Oh, well, that's good for him. He was a nice man. I liked him, not for you, though. I thought he was more Kayley's type."

I thought about that for a moment and shrugged. "Yeah, maybe."

My mom squeezed my hand. "Everything is happening as it is meant to be."

"I guess so."

IT WAS SEVEN O'CLOCK, and I was curled up on the couch reading when my cellphone rang, and I saw it was Ethan. I smiled as I answered it. "I guess you made it to Georgia alright."

"I did. Hey, I want to make this a video call. Hold on a second." I waited for him to switch it, and I connected to the video. "Ah, there you are. A sight for sore eyes."

I rolled mine at him, and he laughed. "How are you feeling?"

"I'm fine. Do not go worrying about me every second of the day. You know I'm tough."

"I do know that. Let me see your stomach."

"What?" I laughed, "Why?"

"Just let me see it. Pull your shirt up and point the phone at your stomach."

"Ethan, come on."

"Riley, do this for me. You kept this secret from me for five weeks, and I'm not there to be a part of this. You are going to have to give me something."

I sighed wearily. "Fine."

I pulled my tank top up and held the phone over my stomach. "See, still as flat as it was when you left this morning."

"Funny. Put the phone closer to your belly."

"Are you really going to talk to my stomach?"

"Yep, I sure am. Now do it."

"You are so bossy." I laughed and put the phone closer to my belly.

"Okay, kid, this is your father. You make sure you behave yourself while I'm gone, and keep your mommy company."

I chuckled, and he started laughing, "You're making our baby seasick with that movement."

I put the phone back in front of me. "Hey, I'll have you know, that little twerp made me throw up two dozen times. He deserves a little seasickness."

Ethan grinned. "I'd tell you that I miss you, but I don't think you'd want to hear it."

"You can tell me." His brows jumped as he leaned back on his bed. "Is that your room?"

"Yep, you want to see it?"

"Yes."

He gave me a quick tour, and by quick, I mean ten seconds of the bed, dresser, closet, and desk.

"Wow, it's like a dorm."

"Pretty much."

"When do you come back?"

"I am here for almost eight more weeks. Think you can live that long without me?" I burst out laughing, but he was laughing too. "It will go fast, and I'm only a phone call away if something happens or you need me."

I gnawed on my bottom lip. "Thank you, Ethan."

"For what?"

"For making this not so scary. I think that with you at my side for this, I won't want to jump off a bridge to save myself."

"You better not. You're going to be alright, Riley. I'm going to be there with you—well, once I get home—I'm going to be there for everything."

"Promise?"

"I promise, baby. Damn, do I promise."

CHAPTER TWENTY-TWO

ETHAN

$\mathcal{I}$ started the next day with a new outlook on life. I didn't try to block thoughts of Riley from my mind, but I did corral them into the corner while I was in class. At lunch, I sent her a text checking on her, and we bantered back and forth for a little while.

Jim, one of my classmates, slapped me on the shoulder. "You look like a different man. Most guys would be depressed for weeks after their mother passed, but you're sitting there grinning."

"Man, I am doing everything I can do, not to think about my mother."

"I wasn't sure you'd come back."

"My father would have kicked my ass if I hadn't. My parents are proud of me and want me to follow through on my dreams. He told me he would have dragged my ass back here if I had refused to come." I chuckled.

"Good parents. I'm sorry about your mom."

"Thanks." I stared at my phone for a moment and then decided I might as well tell him why I was in a good mood. "I got some unexpected good news when I was home."

"Yeah, does that have anything to do with the bruise on your cheek?"

I laughed. "Actually, it does. I found out I'm going to be a father."

Jim leaned back, looking a little shocked, but not quite as much as Sam as she stepped around me and took a seat. "Did you say you're going to have a kid?"

"Yeah, I found out when I was home." I glanced at Sam, hoping that she didn't cause a scene. She was smiling at me, albeit not as widely as she usually did, but she was still smiling —and it looked real.

"Wow! I assume it is with Riley."

"Yep," I replied.

"I didn't know you were in a relationship," Jim said, taking a minute to glance at Sam as if saying, dude, you screwed around on your girl?

"I'm not married, and Riley and I weren't even really a couple."

"Friends with benefits," Sam said with a grin.

"Ah." Jim grinned. "Nice."

"So, what did she say?" Sam asked as she scooped a spoonful of salad into her mouth.

"Said she was going to tell me last weekend, but then Mom passed, and she didn't want to tell me then."

"Who punched you?" Jim asked. "Her father or a brother?"

He laughed. "Her brother, who is actually my best friend."

They both laughed. "So you going to marry her?" Jim asked before he slurped from his soda cup.

"Well, I have no clue about that. I told you we weren't a couple before, and she's not one to be tied down, but Riley said she's willing to try and see how things go."

Sam studied me and then nodded. "Good for her, and you, too, of course."

"Thanks, we'll see. It's going to be rough while I'm here, but we'll figure it out."

"How far along is she?" Sam asked.

"Nine weeks, so she will be sixteen weeks when I see her again."

"Ah." Jim grinned. "That's when things get fun. You're not missing anything now, except the hormones that are on a spin cycle and will make you dizzy, and complaints about not fitting into her clothes."

Sam laughed. "That is pretty accurate."

"Good to know I'm not missing much," I told them.

The rest of the day went smoothly, and that evening after dinner, I sent her a text to see if she was available. She replied that she was, and I called her to do a video chat.

And that's how the next few weeks went. During the day, I worked hard, did my homework, helped in the kitchen, and then spent thirty to sixty minutes chatting with Riley. It was almost like old times, except we talked a lot about the baby, and she wasn't ever drunk.

She was tired a lot, but that was to be expected. Her skin was a soft sun-kissed brown that I envied since I spent my entire summer inside a classroom. Her eyes sparkled, and her skin glowed.

Every night as I turned out the light, I thought about her. Those thoughts led to dreams. Dreams of us seeing each other again when this class was over and dreams of ten years in the future with a house and three kids.

IT HAD BEEN four weeks since I left, and I missed home—not just Riley, but my sisters and my father. I'd had a few days where it had hit me over again that my mom was gone, but I'd told myself not to dwell on that while I was here. It was almost easy pretending that she was still alive, except that I hadn't spoken to her in weeks.

I did keep up with my father and spoke to him twice a week. I'd learned that my siblings were making time to come by and help around the house, and I felt guilty for not being there, but my father told me he understood. I was right where I needed to be. He told me that Riley came by every couple of days and helped tend to my mother's garden. Riley hadn't shared that with me, and I never let her know that I knew. I figured if she wanted me to know, she'd tell me.

The simple fact that she went over there to help meant so much to me. In the last few weeks, Riley and I had gotten closer than we had ever been. I guess that had a lot to do with our nightly talks and the fact that we weren't just falling into bed together. That topic of conversation finally raised its head in the middle of the week.

"I have never been so horny in my life," Riley muttered.

I snickered. "I'm sure you are. I'll be home in on the twenty-seventh, Riley. I'll make sure to take care of those lustful moments."

"Ha! That's the only reason you are looking forward to coming back. The sex, right?"

I laughed. "Oh, sex is a big part of it, Riley, but I just want to be there with you. I can't wait to put my hands on your stomach and feel the changes in your body. Did your boobs get bigger?"

"Oh, my god! They are freaking huge." She set the phone down and ripped off her shirt.

Instant. Erection.

Her breasts were larger, and the bra that she wore was far from sexy, like her favorite black bra. No, this one was plain and white, and her breasts filled it to the extreme, almost pouring out of it as she leaned forward. I was dying to see it up close and personal and had visions of rubbing my cock between them. "See how big they are!"

"Oh, yeah, baby, I see how big they are." She picked the phone up and cocked her head, smirking.

"Your voice got kind of low there, Ethan. You get a little turned on by seeing my big boobs?"

"I'm not going to deny it. I've got a major hard-on right now."

Her smirk got more prominent. "Oh, this could be fun. Why didn't I think of this sooner? We can have phone sex."

I laughed. "Come on, Riley, you don't want to do that, do you?"

Her smiled faded. "I'm kind of desperate right now, Ethan. I haven't had sex with someone in over four weeks."

I chuckled. "I like how you said you hadn't had sex with someone."

"Well, duh! I told you I wouldn't sleep with anyone while I was pregnant."

For a second, I wondered if she had wanted to. That thought kind of killed the mood. "Why does it sound like you've thought about sleeping with someone?"

"Aw, come on, Ethan. You can't say that you've been down there in class with Sam acting like a Boy Scout. I'm not stupid. I know your sexual appetite."

I looked at her, surprised. "You think I'm still sleeping with Sam?"

"Aren't you?"

"No. I'm not Riley. I haven't slept with her since before my mom passed, and that kind of pisses me off that you would think that. I told you that I was all in for us. I want to make this work with you, Riley. You know how I feel about you."

Riley didn't say anything, just stared off in the distance and looked frustrated.

"Riley, what's going on?"

"Nothing."

"Something is going on. Talk to me."

"Ethan, I don't see how this can work. What are we supposed to do, pass the kid back and forth?"

I frowned. "Why can't we live together and raise the baby as a family?"

"Are you going to sell your house and move in here? Because I'm not selling my house."

"Seriously? You want to argue over where we'd live? My house is bigger. It has more room for kids."

"Kids? Did you just say kids? As in plural?" Her voice rose, and I realized that tonight was not the right time for this conversation.

"I meant room for a kid to run around and have their friends over."

"Ethan, what the hell do you think is going to happen between us? Do you think you are going to come home, and we are going to snuggle up in one house and live happily ever after? Have you forgotten that you took a job on the other side of the county, and you're on call twenty-four seven?"

"No, I have not forgotten that, Riley, but have you forgotten that I told you that I was in this for the long haul, and I wanted to make this work? Did you forget that I told you that I loved you?"

"Maybe your love isn't enough," she said softly.

"What the hell does that mean, Riley?" I sat up, feeling extremely frustrated.

She sighed. "Nothing, look I gotta go. I'm tired. I'm going to bed." Before I could say goodbye, she disconnected.

I tossed my phone to the bedside table and growled. "Damn her."

I was too wound up to sit still, so I went out to the common room where a group of people were watching television and playing darts. I grabbed a beer out of the cooler we kept in there and plopped down in a seat.

"You okay?" one of the guys asked.

"Fucking pregnant women," I muttered. "Yeah, I'm fine. She's in one of her mood swings."

Several of the guys laughed. One of them toasted me and wished me luck. I tossed back two beers and tried to relax but still wasn't able to.

I went into the kitchen to find a snack, and Sam slipped up behind me and put her hand on my lower back. "I know something that could ease that stress." She slipped around my body, putting herself between me and the counter. "What do you say?"

Having a woman's body up against mine immediately jacked up my hormones, and my deflated erection began to come back to life.

"You look like you could use a good time." I swallowed as the temptation to take her up on her offer echoed through my mind. "You said it yourself, you two aren't really a couple, and she'll never know."

After our conversation tonight, I wasn't sure if we'd ever be a couple. Sam began to kiss my neck and along my jaw. I clenched my hands to my sides to keep from touching her.

"What do you say, Ethan?" She came closer to my mouth, and damn if I didn't want to take her right there and put her up on the counter to slam into. As her lips touched mine, I put my hands on her shoulders and held her in place as I stepped back. The body in front of me was not the one mine craved. The woman, while a good distraction, was not the one I loved.

"Sorry, Sam. As tempting as that is, I love Riley, and I can't do that to her."

She shrugged with a sigh. "Can't blame a girl for trying one more time." She winked and started to walk away, throwing over her shoulder, "You know where I am if you change your mind."

My eyes landed on her ass as she left the room, and I turned away, frustrated as I hung my head. That was the right decision, but damn if I didn't want to take that back and go after her.

CHAPTER TWENTY-THREE

RILEY

*W*ith summer here and no school, I had my days to screw around. I probably would have been better off being in school because it would have kept my mind occupied. Now it twirled through thoughts of my future, the baby, and Ethan, and I did everything I could to keep myself busy.

I spent more time with my parents' horses and had breakfast with my parents most mornings. I ran errands and visited with friends for lunches. I spent some late mornings, or early afternoons, tending to Rebecca's garden and helping Richard around the house.

By evening I was usually tired, and I'd have a light dinner, then curl up on the couch and read or watch television until it was time to visit with Ethan. After speaking with him was when my mind would start to spiral into the darkness.

Every night we talked, and I enjoyed those conversations. I felt like I had my friend back after a few weeks of us being separated. The problem was, the closer it got to him coming home, the more nervous I became and the more my mind spiraled.

Ethan talked about the future, and I loved the fact that he

wanted to be a part of the baby's life. He really was going to make an incredible father, and I was lucky to have him in that role. I just didn't know how the two of us fit together—or more like—the three of us.

Tonight, he brought up the issue of living together. It wasn't the first time he'd brought it up, but tonight it hit a nerve. I'd already considered this and found the idea had issues. I didn't want to get rid of my house, and I knew he loved his. Yeah, his was bigger with four bedrooms, but mine was perfect for the baby and me.

I tried to fit Ethan into the picture with him living here in my house, and I could, but by doing that, it seemed odd. I couldn't see any of his furniture in my place, and where would his clothes go? I didn't want to give up any drawer space, and I'd have to share my vanity with him. Which wasn't so bad because it was large, and I did have two sinks, but still. I'd been living on my own since I was twenty. It was hard to think of living with someone after that long.

I knew that I was thinking a lot about myself, but I wasn't sure I could think any other way. I just wasn't wired to think like that.

I lay in bed, dwelling over it as my body ached. It wasn't just the changes in my body that caused the ache. It was the sexual need that was in me. I'd always been a sexual person. I always enjoyed sex, and to have sex once in like two months was ridiculous. How I wished I had someone that I could call and ask to come over—someone who was like Ethan—but not Ethan.

The frustrating thing was, I didn't. Ethan had been the only one I trusted in that casual way. I let down my hair with him, and right now, I really needed to let my hair down. I groaned as I rolled over and scissored my legs as the ache grew.

I was so tempted to call Ethan back and get off with him listening, but I'd never done that before. After our last talk, I didn't think it was a good idea. Instead, I reached into my side drawer and pulled out my favorite reliable toy. Who needed a man anyway, when you had a rechargeable pleasure toy?

THE SUMMER HAD WHIZZED BY, and I was back to school today. The kids wouldn't start until next week, but now was the time to get the room in order and start preparing for the new students.

There was in-service training for us that involved our new computer systems, and new testing requirements that our students would have to meet. By the end of the second day, I was already exhausted, and I still had three days to go.

Plus, Friday night, Ethan would be coming home. It was hard to believe that twelve weeks had already gone by for his training, and I was about to hit sixteen weeks pregnant. I had a cute little baby bump, and even though Ethan had tried to get me to show it to him, I had refused.

I wanted him to see it for the first time once he got home. I was hoping that as soon as he did arrive home, that he would come over, sweep me off my feet, and take me right to bed. Oh, the thought of finally having sex again was a heady one. I'd been dreaming about it for weeks.

Last night when we had spoken, Ethan had gotten serious, and his sigh had washed over me. "I miss you, Riley."

"I miss you, too," I replied. I did miss him. I missed having sex and being able to laugh with him. I missed how he knew me so well and how I didn't have to explain myself to him as I did to so many others.

"Do you?" he asked huskily.

I laughed. "Of course, I miss you, Ethan."

"How do you miss me?"

I frowned. "What do you mean, how do I miss you? I just do."

"Riley, when I think of you, my heart aches. I want to hold you so damn bad that my arms tingle just thinking about it. I can close my eyes and imagine your perfume and the scent of your shampoo as your hair fans out on my chest. I can see your beautiful eyes even when mine are closed, and I want to pull you to me and never let you go. That's how I miss you, Riley. You are always on my mind, and I can't wait to get back to you."

I stared at him, at a loss as to what to say. How did I feel about him? "I miss you, too, Ethan."

"But not like that."

"Ethan, I don't know what you want me to say here. You know who I am and how I am. I'm not as poetic as you are, and I know you love me."

"But you still don't love me, do you?"

"Ethan. I do love you."

"How?"

I laughed. "Oh, my god, Ethan! Come on. You know that I love you. You know that I would do anything for you. I'm having your damn kid, for God's sake!"

"Whoa, are you saying you're only having it for me?"

"No! That's not what I meant. Look, Ethan, I'm tired, and I'm cranky, and I want to go to bed. We can rehash this when you get home, okay. Let's just talk about all of this then, alright?"

"Fine, night, Riley." He hung up before I could even say good night.

"Men!" I shouted to the room as I got up and turned off the lights before I headed upstairs.

I hated that he kept pushing this, and I knew that we were going to butt heads when he came home. But at least we could do that face-to-face, and I could entice him to my bed to sate my wild hormones when we were finished.

By the end of the week, I was whipped, and Ethan sent me a message saying his flight was going to be late. I told him that I'd see him on Saturday because I needed sleep. It also gave me one more night of peace before I knew he would be turning the screws on me.

Saturday morning, I was in the kitchen making a cup of coffee—sadly decaf, but at least it was coffee—when my doorbell rang. I glanced at the clock and saw that it was almost eight. I did not doubt that it was Ethan, and I actually grinned as I rushed to the door.

The thought that he was on the other side of the door, and he wouldn't be flying a thousand miles away again, made me happy. I pulled open the door, found him standing there with a pastry bag in his hands, and launched myself into his arms.

I shocked him as he stepped back to steady us and chuckled. "Nice to see you too," he said as he hugged me tightly. I leaned back, staring into his face, and found myself drifting my eyes over his features as if I was searching for changes in him.

He didn't say anything, just let me stare at him, and I cupped his face and went up on my tiptoes. Our lips were only half an inch apart as we stared at one another. He was letting me take control of this situation, and I did. I pressed my lips to his, wrapping my arms tightly around his neck. His arms banded around my back, and he tipped his head further to the side to deepen the kiss.

I missed his kisses. God, did I miss his kisses. We were breathless when we pulled away from one another.

"Welcome back," I said as I grinned at him.

"It's nice to be home." He held up the bag. "I bought you your favorite sandwich."

At the mention of food, I snagged the bag as he chuckled and followed me into the house. I was in the kitchen, taking the food out as Ethan stood off to the side. I glanced at him and found him staring at my belly. Instantly, my hand went to it and cupped the front bulge.

His eyes came to mine, and he smiled. "Let me see it."

If anyone else had asked, I would have laughed at them, but

this little one in my belly was his. I lifted my shirt, and Ethan stepped forward and went to his knees, putting his hands on my growing sides. "Hey, little one. It's your father. Now you are going to get used to me talking so that you recognize me. I'm home, and I'm not leaving you alone again."

He leaned forward and kissed my belly, and I jerked. Ethan looked up at me. "What? Did I hurt you?"

"No! The baby kicked. Just as you kissed my belly, he kicked."

"He?"

"Or she?" I laughed. "That's not the point. Ethan, that was only the second time I'd felt the baby move."

"Really?"

"Yes. The first time, I wasn't sure if I had felt it, but there was no doubt that I just felt it now."

Ethan laughed and began talking to my belly again. "You're letting Mommy know that you can hear me, right? You keep doing that, little one."

There was another flutter in my belly, and I brushed the hair back on his forehead as he leaned forward and hugged me, putting his cheek to my stomach and holding me tightly.

He leaned back, laughing. "Sounds like both you and baby are hungry."

"We are. Thanks for breakfast." I gathered two plates and put our sandwiches on them while he made a cup of coffee, and I retrieved a bowl of cut fruit from the fridge.

It wasn't lost on me that we moved around the kitchen together well, and even though we hadn't seen each other in weeks, it wasn't uncomfortable. As we ate, Ethan told me about the last day of his class and graduation and then his flight home.

When he finished, he leaned on the table and stared at me. "How are you doing? I mean, really? Is there anything that I can do to help? Anything you need me to do? Just name it. I haven't been here, but I am now, and I'm willing to help."

"Willing, huh?" I raised a brow.

He chuckled. "Well, that depends on what you have in mind."

I stood up, whipping my shirt off and tossing it to the side. "You can take me to bed and sate these horrible pregnancy hormones."

His eyes locked on my chest, and he licked his lips before he was on his feet and taking hold of my face. He kissed me with a fierceness that I felt in the pit of my stomach, and I clung to him and whimpered. I needed this man to make love to me. God, did I need this man.

"Riley," he murmured between kisses as he collected me in his arms and began to carry me to the stairs.

Upstairs, Ethan laid me on the bed as if I were the most precious piece of cargo and might break. He stared at me for a moment, then removed his shirt, pants, and shoes before lying beside me, cupping my face and staring at me like I was the most important thing in the world to him.

I wanted to be that person, but I just wasn't sure if I could give that feeling back to him. Instead of facing that, I leaned forward and captured his lips, all thought of conversation gone as my body welcomed his back.

CHAPTER TWENTY-FOUR

ETHAN

*H*aving Riley welcome me the way she did was all I could have asked for, and seeing her growing belly as she moved around her kitchen almost brought me to tears. I was overcome with emotion, although I was able to keep it under wraps.

All through breakfast, I'd wanted to put her into my lap and kiss her again. I wanted to claim her body as mine, connect to her in that intimate way that started our family in the first place. Riley was stunning, and while she'd had a few bad weeks at first, she seemed to be doing well now.

Making love to Riley today was different somehow. Even though we were both in a hurry, we took our time. It wasn't a rushed reunion. It was more like we were slowly trying to cover all the time we missed. There were more touches, more kisses, longer caresses, and a whole lot of intense stares.

When we finished, I held her to me for a long time. "You sated now?"

"For the moment," she said and laughed. "I could use a shower and another breakfast."

I glanced at my watch. "Actually, I told my father I'd be over there for lunch. You want to join us?"

"You should probably go by yourself. I wouldn't want to invade the family."

I tilted her chin toward me. "Riley, you are part of the family. Not just because you're a Young, but because you're carrying a piece of our family."

"There is that."

"So, how about I wash your back and then we head over to my father's?"

"I might be talked into that, but I think we need to kill some more time," she said sassily as she climbed out of bed, and I stared at her profile as she left the bedroom. Damn, her body was sexy as hell. My erection was already growing as I rushed to follow her.

In the shower, I stood behind her, one hand on her belly, the other on a breast, and my mouth on her neck. Our shower took about three times as long as it should have, but neither of us seemed to be in a rush.

We were a little later getting to my father's than planned, but I wasn't worried about it. It was going to be a laid-back affair with just a few of us, but when we pulled down the driveway, I realized it was a whole lot more than that. There must have been a dozen cars outside, and I tensed.

"What's going on?"

Riley grinned next to me. "Nothing, everyone is just welcoming you home."

"You knew about this?"

She rolled her eyes. "Of course, I knew about it. It was my job to keep you busy until it was time."

"Oh," I laughed. "That's why we had such a long shower, huh?"

"Well, that and I really need to work off more sexual energy."

I parked my truck and leaned toward her. "Baby, you can work that off with me anytime you want."

She laughed and opened her door. After I met her at the front of my truck, she grinned. "You might not want to say that. I'm rather insatiable right now."

Damn, if my dick didn't start to wake up again. I grabbed her around the shoulders, pulling her back against me and whispering in her ear. "We could go climb in the back seat of my truck and take care of that again. I don't think they'd miss us."

"Uncle Ethan!" Marisol yelled as she came around the side of the house and saw me. She ran over to us and jumped into my arms, and I could imagine my own child doing that. The thought filled my heart to the point that it might explode.

"How are you doing, Miss Marisol? Are you keeping your nose clean? Staying out of trouble with the police?"

She giggled as I tickled her. "Yes!" I put her down on the ground, and she turned to me. "Do you know that Aunt Riley has a baby in her tummy?"

"Yes, I sure do," I said to her. "What do you think about that?"

"I can't wait. I want her to have a little girl so that I have someone I can dress up like my dolls."

I chuckled. "Well, we'll have to see about that."

She waved a quick goodbye and raced away as I put my arm around Riley's shoulders, and we headed toward the back of the house.

We were almost to the back when I spun Riley around and took her face. "I love you."

She froze for a second, then smiled. "I know, Ethan. Come on, let's go see everyone."

Before I let her pull me away, I kissed her deeply and then rested my forehead against hers.

"Hey! You two haven't gotten enough of that since last night? Cut that crap out. That's how you two got in trouble in the first place." I laughed as I took Riley's hand and grinned at Cara.

"Oh, you're funny." Riley slipped away from me the minute I let go of her hand while my family converged on me. After they were done, the Youngs were there, and a few other friends from the police force. It was good to see them, and it was weird knowing that I wouldn't be working with them anymore—at least not directly. Even though I'd been with the county detectives for officially fourteen weeks, I'd barely started there before I left for training. It seemed surreal to be going there on Monday and not back to my old department.

It was a perfect afternoon. The weather was excellent for end of August, and everyone was in good spirits. Charlotte and Wes announced that they were expecting, and I noticed Roxy and Henley staring at each other with conspiratorial smiles. I had a feeling that they were going to be next to announce that.

The weirdest part about the whole afternoon was when I grabbed a beer out of the cooler and looked up to find Joe Newman there. He approached me, his hand out. "Ethan, congrats on your class. I know that things didn't start out so well between us, but I hope we can start over."

I shook his hand. "Thanks." I glanced around to find Riley and saw her laughing with Charlotte and Roxy on the other side of the patio. "Who invited you?"

"I'm here as a guest to Carmen. I guess she didn't tell you that we've started seeing each other."

"My sister, Carmen?"

Joe chuckled. "Yeah, is that going to be a problem?"

I searched for Carmen; she was watching me, and I saw the nervous look in her eye. "You're dating my sister now." I nodded slowly.

He shifted on his feet as if he expected me to throw a punch. Instead, I laughed. "Sure, go for it." I slapped him on the arm and walked past him, laughing.

I didn't care who he dated as long as he was far away from Riley. Speaking of her, I made a beeline to her and put my arm around her shoulders. I was flying on a high, and I was ready to continue it.

"Hey! Can I get everyone's attention?" I called out as I pulled Riley closer to my side.

"What are you doing?" Riley laughed as she stood beside me.

I smiled down at her and winked. "So, first, I want to thank you guys for coming today. This was a great surprise, and I'm jealous as hell of the tans that all of you have since I spent the entire summer locked in a room with twenty other people."

"Yeah, you do look a little pasty there, Ethan," Evan joked, and everyone laughed.

"Yeah, this is the first year your tan is better than mine," I replied back to Evan in jest, and then I scanned the group. "I'm pretty sure that everybody is now aware that Riley and I are expecting a baby in another twenty-four weeks or so."

A few whistles and yells filled the air, and I inhaled deeply and hesitated just a fraction of a second. Then I glanced at my father smiling at me, and I realized that I couldn't waste a minute longer. I turned to Riley as I started to drop to my knee.

"Ethan?" she asked me as she cocked her head. "Ethan, what the hell are you doing?"

"Riley Young, you and I have had a roller coaster of a relationship since we were in high school, but I know without a doubt that I love you and would do anything for you or our child. I know that while you are probably freaking out right this minute, I also know that this is the right thing to do. In front of our families, especially in front of your family, I want everyone to see my pledge to you and to our child."

"Ethan," Riley said so softly that I doubted anyone else could hear it. Or maybe they could because my heart was hammering so loudly in my ears that I could be blocking out the sound.

"Riley, let me be right there with you through everything that you and our child go through. Let me give you everything that you deserve." I licked my lips and inhaled slowly as I pulled a ring out of my pocket. "Riley Young, will you marry me?"

Riley stared down at me and then glanced at the ring. Her hand went to her mouth, and tears began to fill her eyes. I thought I had her there, thought that by announcing to everyone here how much I loved her, it would be enough.

But it wasn't.

Riley stepped back, pulling her hand from mine as she shook her head back and forth slowly. She took a second step as her hand dropped to her side, and then she was turning and rushing away. Henley, who had been standing behind her, grabbed her, but she jerked out of his hold and began to run toward the front of the house.

I watched her go and then got off my knee as I stared at the ring. It had been a gamble, and one I had hoped would pay off. I thought that maybe if I did it in front of our families, she would have said yes so that she didn't upset anyone. Obviously, I had been seriously wrong.

Cara and Candy came to my side, murmuring that it would be okay, and I saw Henley run after his sister.

Wes joined us and joked loudly, "Damn pregnancy hormones. She's even more of a flake than she normally is." A few people laughed and looked at me nervously. Wes paused next to me. "Give her time to calm down. Even if she says no later, the fact that you asked—and I know you meant every word that you said—carries weight in our family. I'm sure she will come around in time." He patted me on the back.

"You should go check on her," Cara suggested.

"I'm not sure she wants to see me right now," I replied sadly.

"I'm pretty sure she does. I think she just didn't want the audience. Go talk to her, get her to tell you where her head is and why she ran away, Ethan. If you love her as you say, you need to do that."

"Alright," I replied in a huff and took off to find her and her brother.

I saw them talking near his truck, and he was holding the door open. I ran over to them just as she was climbing in. "Riley, don't go."

"Ethan." She swiped the tears from her cheek. "I can't believe you just did that! How could you do that?"

"Come out of there. We need to talk."

"No! I don't want to talk to you! I can't believe you just did that."

Henley put his hand on my shoulder, and I turned and glared at him. "So help me, God, Henley. If you don't let go of me and let me talk to your sister, I'm going to knock you on your ass!"

"Whoa!" Henley said and threw up his hands. "You both need to calm the hell down."

I reached into the truck and picked Riley up as she squealed, "What are you doing?"

"If you want to go home, then I will take you home."

"Fine, I don't care how I get there! I just want to be away from this," she hissed at me.

"Are you sure, Ry? I can take you home," Henley said, and I stared daggers at him.

"No, he should take me home so he can explain to me why he got this stupid idea in his head that we should get married. Put me down! I can walk."

I set her down, and she pushed away and stalked to my truck. Once I was behind the wheel, she rounded on me.

"How dare you do that! Ethan, what the hell were you thinking?"

"I was thinking about the fact that I love you, Riley! That I want our child to have a family!" I turned the truck on and started to back up to turn around.

"We don't have to be married to be a family! Jesus! That was the stupidest thing you have ever done!" She threw her hands in the air.

"Why was it stupid, Riley? I love you! I love our child! What about that is stupid?" I pulled out on the main road.

"Everything! Why would you do that in front of all those people! Oh my god! You embarrassed us both!" she screamed. "I can't marry you, Ethan!"

I stepped on the gas, my blood pounding in my veins as the anger between us grew. "Why can't you, Riley?"

"Because I can't!"

"Why? That's not a reason, Riley. I want a fucking reason!"

"Because I don't love you! Jesus, Ethan! I don't love you like that! Don't you understand that? I can't love you like that!"

I stared at her, and I knew I should have my eyes on the road, but I couldn't look away. She'd never said that she didn't love me, not like that.

Suddenly, her eyes enlarged as she looked past me, and she screamed, "Ethan!"

I turned to look out the front window, my eyes passing over a stop sign. A stop sign that I had completely forgotten about. Before I could think anything else, a vehicle slammed into my door, and the world went black.

CHAPTER TWENTY-FIVE

RILEY

*T*his morning when Ethan arrived, I'd been slightly overwhelmed at the feelings that he evoked in me. Making love to him had been somewhat different than I'd remembered, or perhaps my memory was skewed because I was sober now. How long had it been since we'd had sex and I'd been sober? I honestly couldn't remember—maybe years.

I knew about the party, and I kept him busy until it was time to be there. When he had invited me to join them, I had to pretend that I knew nothing. In fact, I'd acted as if I'd be a third wheel, but that's not how he saw it.

I was already part of his family because of the little one I carried. Henley and I had probably been the closest to that family growing up, but why did Ethan's statement mean something more to me?

I didn't want to look too much into it, but as the day progressed, I found myself eyeing him more closely. Sometimes, my heart would falter in my chest at the sight of him laughing or talking to someone. If he caught my eye and smiled, my knees felt a little weak, and I had no clue why.

Which is one of the reasons I had avoided him for most of

the party. Instead, I spent a lot of time talking to Charlotte about her pregnancy, and Roxy let us in on a little secret that she and Henley were trying, too. How awesome would it be for my child to have cousins so close in age?

My cousins had lived far away, and while we'd been friendly over the years, we weren't close. I was way closer to the Winston kids than I had ever been to my blood cousins. In a way, I feel that I had missed out.

As it was, my child would have three older ones: Tonya, Tyler, and Marisol, and now Charlotte's baby. It was rather exciting. So exciting that when Ethan pulled me in front of everyone and started talking, I was smiling. Life was good. Life was getting better every day.

Ethan was home, and he would get to share in the joy of our child growing. We'd get to know one another, and maybe I'd come to understand the feelings I had for him. Perhaps I'd love him, and someday we could turn this into something else.

Only as I listened to him and he dropped to his knee, I began to panic! No! Ethan, oh god! Don't do this here! He couldn't be proposing to me in front of everyone!

"Riley Young, you and I have had a roller coaster of a relationship since we were in high school, but I know without a doubt that I love you and would do anything for you or our child. I know that while you are probably freaking out right this minute, I also know that this is the right thing to do."

You think? I was shaking in my shoes. My voice caught in my throat. If I could have spoken, I would have told him to stop!

"In front of our families, especially in front of your family, I want everyone to see my pledge to you and to our child."

Was he just committing himself to our little family? No! He was asking me to marry him! Ethan—no! "Ethan," I breathed out.

"Riley, let me be right there with you through everything

that you and our child go through. Let me give you everything that you deserve."

I wanted to cry, to yank my hand away from him, but I was frozen as I stared down at him. Please don't ask me Ethan, please!

"Riley Young, will you marry me?"

He lifted the ring and held it up to me, and I covered my mouth to hold back the sob. How could he do this? My flight response kicked in, and I began to move away, pulling my hand from his and watching his emotions crushed under the weight of my movement. I didn't want to crush him, didn't want him to hurt. I wanted him to take this back. I wasn't ready—I wasn't ready.

I turned and ran, heard my name called from someplace, but I couldn't look back as I jogged around the side of the house and looked for a way out of here.

A hand landed on my shoulder, and I almost screamed. I didn't want to hash this out with Ethan here. It was already bad enough that he had embarrassed us both. We didn't need to continue the show.

"What the hell are you doing?" my brother hissed. "Why did you run away from him?"

"I can't marry him, Lee! He's only proposing because I'm pregnant."

"Riley, he loves you!"

"Get me out of here, Henley. I need to go lie down. I don't feel well."

He took my arm and led me to his truck. "Ethan asked you to marry him because he loves you. Not out of some weird sense of obligation."

"Henley, just take me home."

He held the door open, and I was sitting down when Ethan showed up. "Riley, don't go."

"Ethan, I can't believe you just did that! How could you do that?"

"Come out of there. We need to talk."

"No! I don't want to talk to you! I can't believe you just did that."

I heard him threaten my brother, and I didn't want to cause more of an issue, so I let him pick me up and take me to his truck—as long as he was taking me home. I didn't care who did. I just wanted to go lie down.

As Henley spoke to me, I decided that now might be a good time for Ethan to explain and the only way I'd let him was if we were without an audience. I stalked away from him and got in his truck.

The minute the door was closed, I snapped at him, "How dare you do that! Ethan, what the hell were you thinking?"

"I was thinking about the fact that I love you, Riley! That I want our child to have a family!"

I was livid, but at the same time, there was another feeling there, and I wasn't sure what that was. "We don't have to be married to be a family! Jesus! That was the stupidest thing you have ever done!"

"Why was it stupid, Riley? I love you! I love our child! What about that is stupid?"

"Everything! Why would you do that in front of all those people! Oh my god! You embarrassed us both! I can't marry you, Ethan!"

This was a bad idea, the two of us screaming at each other over why I felt we shouldn't get married. Didn't he understand that I didn't know how to do a relationship? Didn't he know how scared I was that it would fail and that my heart would be broken?

I hadn't been in love with anyone since I was a teenager. I protected my heart against it being broken. I didn't know why I did that, but I did. It could be because I saw so many of my friends get walked on by people in their lives, and I didn't want that to happen to me.

"Why can't you, Riley?"

"Because I can't!"

"Why? That's not a reason, Riley. I want a fucking reason!"

I blinked slowly. The only thing I could do was push him as far away from me as I could, and the words came out. "Because I don't love you! Jesus, Ethan! I don't love you like that! Don't you understand that? I can't love you like that!"

His eyes locked on to mine as we barreled down the street, and I saw the words register in his mind just as something caught my eye past him. I shifted my eyes and saw a box truck barreling toward us.

I only had time for one word as I began to brace myself. "Ethan!" I watched his head turn as the front grill of the truck slammed into his pickup, and then the noise exploded around me, glass struck me, and my body was bounced around inside the cab of his truck for a few seconds as I felt like I was in a corkscrew and turning, over and over.

When the truck came to a rest, we were on our side, and I was the closest to the ground. I blinked, feeling like I was going to throw up. I could move my hands, my arms, turn my head—ouch, that hurt.

I tried to reach for Ethan but couldn't find him. I glanced to my left, and the seat was empty. "Ethan! Ethan!" Panic exploded in my gut, and I started screaming, "Ethan!" I looked all around the inside of the truck like I knew he was supposed to be here, and then I noticed that the front windshield was torn outward, and there was something red on the edges of the glass.

I tried to get my seat belt off, tried to get out of the truck, but I was stuck. I heard voices coming closer, and someone came to me. "Ethan! Where is Ethan?"

"He's out here. He's alive. Help is on the way," a man said.

"Don't let him be alone! Go to him! Don't let him be alone!" I told him, pushing his hand away from me.

"It's okay. My wife is with him. She's a nurse. Are you okay?"

"I think so, but I'm pregnant." Suddenly the most substantial wave of fear I had ever felt washed over me as my hand went to my stomach. "Oh, my god! My baby!"

"It's okay. Help is coming. We will get you out, and you and your baby will be okay."

I heard a few tires squeal as if someone applied the brakes hard, and then I heard Henley's voice, and I started to cry. "Riley!" Huntley's voice was there too, along with Wesley and Cara.

Hunt came to me. "Are you okay?"

"I don't know! How is Ethan?" Hunt looked over his shoulder, and I heard Cara scream. Hunt winced. "We need to get you out of there, but I don't want to move you until we have a collar on you. What hurts?"

I wanted to scream that my heart hurt. It's breaking on the road in front of us. Why had I said that to him? Why hadn't I just told him yes and then spoken to him later in private?

"Everything hurts right now." I heard Wes talking behind him, his voice grave but in control, although none of the words made sense to me, and Henley was with him answering back. Cara was crying, and I was going crazy locked in the cab of his pickup. I needed to see Ethan! I had to see him.

Sirens could be heard in the distance, and Henley came to me. "Are you okay?"

There was blood on his hands, and I grabbed them. "Hen, is he okay?"

His face went blank. "We are doing everything we can."

"Is he going to die?" The words squeaked out of my mouth.

"I don't know, Ry. It's not good."

I put my hands to my face and sobbed into them as Hunt and

Hen tried to console me. This was all my fault. If he died, I would never forgive myself.

Hen kept looking over his shoulder, and I heard voices talking about Ethan being put on a chopper. People started working on the truck to stabilize it so that they could get me out of it safely, and I saw feet everywhere as I looked at the world sideways from my vantage point.

The chopper was overhead and landing in a field off to the side. They weren't going to get me out in time for me to see him. I might never see him again, never speak to him again.

As they pulled me to a rigid board and out of the truck, I peered through slitted eyelids to watch the helicopter take off. The last words I said to him were like a knife in my own chest as they echoed through my mind. *I don't love you like that! Don't you understand that? I can't love you like that!*

CHAPTER TWENTY-SIX

RILEY

They took me to the local hospital where they had an excellent obstetrics department because they were worried about the baby. My injuries appeared superficial, they said. Ethan was flown to Summersville where they had a trauma facility. I knew he was in good hands, had been since Wes arrived at the scene. He was an emergency room doctor, and I knew that he would do his best to save Ethan.

How bad had Ethan been? Hadn't Henley said they would do everything that they could? Did that mean that Ethan was going to die?

I stared at the wall of the hospital room I was in—the monitors on my side beeping, a tight band wrapped around my belly, measuring the fetal movements. The door opened, and my parents rushed to my side.

"Riley," my mother cried. "We heard the accident from the house!" She wiped at her eyes. "Hen, Hunt, Wes, and Cara all ran to a car and took off after you. Cara called back and told us what had happened. You are lucky to be alive." She brushed the hair from my head.

I was lucky to be alive? Did that mean he wasn't?

"Mom? Is Ethan—"

"They are working on him. His family is at the hospital now. A couple of his friends from the police station drove them lights and siren over there. I spoke to Coral a few minutes ago. All I know is that they are working on him."

I closed my eyes. "I'm sorry."

"Sweetheart, there is nothing to be sorry for," my mother assured me, but she was wrong, and I started to cry.

"Nothing to be sorry for? Mom! It was my fault! If I hadn't freaked out—if I hadn't told him—" I paused, not able to say the words out loud again.

"Say what, honey? What did you say?"

I shook my head, wincing from the pain. Even though nothing was specifically wrong with me, my entire body hurt from tensing up and being thrown around like a rag doll.

"Nothing." I let the tears course down my cheeks. "If he dies, it will be my fault, Mom. I'll never forgive myself."

"Riley, he'll be okay, and it wasn't your fault. It happened. It was horrible, but it wasn't your fault."

"How could it not be my fault? I ran from him after he proposed, and we were screaming at each other in the car! I told him that I didn't love him, Mom! And a second later, we were hit! Those were the last words that he heard from me!" I started to sob, my entire body shaking as my mother clung to one hand, and my father rubbed my leg. "Those were my last words."

THE NURSE ENDED up giving me a sedative—against my wishes —and I was knocked out for a while. When I woke up, I was groggy and slightly hungry. I opened my eyes to find Henley sitting in my room, staring at the television that was on silent. He glanced my way as I moved.

"Hey, how are you feeling?"

"I'm okay. I think I'm hungry." I glanced around. "Where am I?"

"They moved you out of the ER. You're going to have to stay the night."

I started to sit up. "No! I need to get to Summersville and see Ethan."

Henley put his hand up, and I noted his face. It was sad, almost mournfully so. "Lee," I shook my head, "Don't you tell me he's dead!"

"He's alive, Riley, but he's in a coma."

"What happened to him?"

Henley looked at my monitor. "I'll tell you, but you need to remain calm. If you get overly agitated again, they will put you back under. She's stressed, and we need to keep her calm."

"Her?"

He gave me a small smile. "Sorry, I didn't mean to let the cat out of the bag."

My hand went to my belly. "I'm having a girl?"

"Yes, and she is okay, but we need to keep her that way, Riley."

"Tell me about Ethan." I rubbed my belly as I thought about the fact that I was having a girl. Oh, shit!

Henley took my hand. "You know he was thrown from the truck while it rolled. The truck rolled three times. You were lucky to have your seat belt on, but Ethan hadn't put his on." He shook his head and stared off into space for a moment.

I squeezed his hand to bring him back. "He was hurt really bad, Ry. His skull was cracked, his arm almost completely torn off. One of his legs was broken."

I thought I would puke, but I forced myself to remain calm— or as calm as I could. Henley looked at the monitor and squeezed my hand again. "You need to take a few breaths, Riley."

I forced stuttered breaths into my lungs and out again as I pictured Ethan lying on the ground, torn and bleeding. Tears ran like rivers from my eyes, and I took another stuttered breath as the alarm went off on one of my machines. A nurse popped her head into the room, but I saw spots in front of me as the image of Ethan bleeding grew bigger and bigger in my mind.

I heard the nurse speaking to Henley, and then I was floating off, and the image thankfully began to vanish.

DANIELLA WAS THERE when I woke up later. I knew it before I even opened my eyes. Her fingers were flying over her keyboard. The woman could write in any circumstance, any place she deemed necessary.

"Hey," I called to her as I reached for the water glass on my tray.

She set her laptop quickly to the side and moved the tray closer to me. "How are you feeling?"

"How is Ethan?"

"I've been told I am not allowed to speak about him because every time someone does, you stress that little girl out." She smiled to soften her words.

"Is he still alive?"

She nodded sadly. "He's fighting, Riley."

I glanced at the clock. "How is it only six at night? It seems like this day just won't end."

Daniella took my hand and squeezed it. "It's Monday night at six."

"What? Are you saying that I've been out for two days?"

"Yeah, well, they kept you sedated for a little over twenty-four hours to calm down the baby and your uterus, and then you woke up late yesterday and got all upset, so they put you back down for another twenty-four hours to be safe. But your vitals are much better, and the baby seems to be out of the woods now."

At least that was good. "I think Hen said that Ethan was in a coma. Is he still in one?"

She nodded. "Yeah, for now, but let's not talk about that anymore. If things are still going smooth for you, they will let you out of the hospital tomorrow."

"Good, then I can go see Ethan."

"I don't think that's a good idea, Riley. I'm pretty sure the doctors are going to put you on bed rest."

"I don't care. I have to go see Ethan."

"Right now, the only people that can see him are his family, and only one person at a time for a few minutes every hour." She winced as she looked at my monitor. "Ry, you need to calm down, or they are going to put you out again."

I glared at the monitor and closed my eyes, taking a deep breath. My monitor stopped beeping at me after a moment. The nurse stepped into the room and eyed me carefully.

"I'm okay. I'm calming myself down. No need to knock me out again."

She chuckled. "Good to hear that. You ready to eat?"

"Yes, I'm starved."

She left saying that she'd have some food delivered in a few minutes. "So other than a few bruises and sore muscles, I'm okay?"

She nodded happily. "Yes, God was watching out for you, Riley. You were unharmed. Thankfully you had your seat belt on. I can't believe he didn't."

"He was angry. We were fighting. He wasn't even looking at the road. He was looking at me when we came to that intersection."

"Oh, Riley, I'm so sorry, but don't blame yourself. Ethan is a cop. He knows how dangerous driving can be. That accident wasn't your fault."

"If I had just accepted his proposal, none of this would have happened, Dani."

She seemed to consider her words for a moment. "Why didn't you?"

"Because I'm stupid, and I was scared, and, oh, my god! Dani! I screwed up so badly."

She sat on the edge of the bed. "No, you can fix it later. He loves you."

"I told him that I didn't love him. That was the last thing I said to him."

"You don't love him? How can you not love him, Riley? That man was made for you. You two are the perfect couple. Every time you look at one another, everyone can see the sparks between you. You seem to be the only one that can't see them. Or maybe you don't want to see them because you are scared. I get it. Damn, do I get it, but you can't be afraid to love."

"How can I not, Dani?"

"Because if you don't let yourself love, then you will spend the rest of your life in one meaningless relationship after another. These last few weeks, you have been so happy talking about the baby and things you and Ethan discuss. I don't think you even realize how much you love him. You need him in your life."

"And if he dies? What am I supposed to do then?" I said. "I'll be carrying around the guilt of those last words that I spoke. I was in panic mode, and I wanted him to back off. I didn't mean it."

"You didn't mean it when you said you didn't love him?"

"No." I shook my head, and as I did, I knew I was finally being honest with myself. I did love Ethan. Holy crap, I loved the man so damn much. I knew it that morning when we'd made love; I knew it when he went to his knee in front of me, and when he removed me from Henley's truck, and when I told him that I didn't.

I grabbed Dani's hand with both of mine. "Dani, I screwed up so bad. I love him. I do love him. I need Ethan! He can't die. I have to see him and tell him that I'm sorry and that I love him."

"When the doctor says it's okay, then you will. Right now, you need to rest and eat, and then we will come up with a plan to get him back."

"You'll help me?"

She grinned. "Only if you let me use it in a book later."

I laughed as the door opened and someone walked in with a tray of food. I responded to Dani as she set it down. "Deal!"

CHAPTER TWENTY-SEVEN

ETHAN

I was aware of a few sounds and my own heart beating for a time, but nothing made sense. I recognized a couple of voices, but words seemed distorted and as if they were coming from a far distance. I tried to remember where I was and what was happening, but I couldn't.

For a long time, I floated. In what I wasn't sure. I didn't think I was floating in the water—I didn't feel wet—but I didn't think it was air either. How could I float? Where was everyone else? Had I died? Was I in some limbo between life and death?

As if thinking about death released the memory, I saw Riley's face. Her beautiful face morphed from angry to fearful in a second, and I turned my head in my mind to see a truck coming at us.

Had that truck killed me? Was Riley alright? Was our baby alright? I tried to fight myself to the surface, but I couldn't. Something was holding me down, and the stronger it pulled, the more I fought it. Other memories swamped my mind, distorted memories of other family moments. Funerals and flowers, and I thought of my mother. If I had died, wouldn't she be here waiting for me?

Had I been such a bastard in life that I was heading to purgatory? Was this my hell? Was I going to have to float here for eternity with my own fucked-up memories? Please, no!

I had to get back. I had a life to live, a family that needed me. I had a child, or had I killed the baby as I'd killed myself? Was Riley alive? Riley couldn't die! What had I done?

I DON'T KNOW how long it was before I could flutter my eyelids, and they opened to a bright room. I squinted against the lights, and someone was in my face. "Ethan, I'm Rose, stay calm for me, and I'll get that tube out of your throat."

She messed with a machine beside me and then leaned back over. "I want you to cough as hard as you can when I tell you." She removed the tape from my mouth and started to pull the tube. It was like someone had reached down my throat and was pulling my lungs up with it.

"Cough," she told me, and I forced myself to cough as hard as I could, which didn't seem like enough. My entire body ached, and I felt weak while my shoulder and head pounded.

As soon as the tube was out of the way, she shifted the bed so that I was sitting up slightly. My eyes shifted around the room to find my father and Cara off to the side. They stepped forward immediately, both of them crying.

"Hey," I breathed and winced at the sound of my froggy voice.

"Your throat is going to hurt for a few days, but that will go away. I'll have the doctor come in to speak with you in a few minutes. How are you feeling right now?" the nurse asked me.

"Like I got hit by a truck."

She glanced at my father and sister.

"Ethan, do you remember what happened?"

I hesitated, did I? I wasn't sure. My mind was a jumbled mess.

"You were in an accident," my father said. "You *were* hit by a truck."

"So that memory was real." Suddenly I remembered something else. "Riley? The baby?" I asked as the nurse turned off a switch to quiet the beeping.

"Riley and the baby are fine," my father said, and I noticed my sister purse her lips. "They are home resting, and they are fine."

"Who is taking care of them?"

"Ethan, don't worry about that," Cara said a little harshly. "The last thing you should worry about is her."

"Cara," my father growled at her.

"What are you talking about, Cara?"

"She's the reason you were in that accident. If she hadn't been such a selfish bitch, you would be fine."

"It wasn't her fault," I told her.

My father looked at her sternly. "Enough, Cara. Not another word." He paused, "We know it wasn't her fault, and it wasn't yours either, Ethan. Accidents happen. That's all it was. You're back with us now. That's all that matters."

Back with them now? How close had I come to not being here? I learned that answer a few minutes later when the doctor arrived.

"Ethan, it's good to have you with us. We weren't sure if you'd make it."

"What's the verdict, Doc? Am I going to recover to normal?"

"Well, we have a lot of tests to run, but the fact that you are sitting up, talking in full sentences, and seem to understand what is being said to you is a plus. Your skull was fractured, and you had a couple of brain bleeds. We had to go in and pick out a few fragments too and reattach your arm."

I glanced at my left arm and saw a brace around it. It looked like something you'd wear if you had a sprain, not if it had been severed. "Reattach it?"

"Yeah, it was almost sheared off, but we believe with a lot of physical therapy, you will recover completely with that. Wes Young had a friend of his flown in to complete the surgery. Best damn orthopedic surgeon I've ever seen. That arm might work better now than it did before. Can you wiggle your fingers?"

I looked down at my hand and concentrated. My fingers wiggled a little bit, and I knew he wasn't joking about how much rehab it was going to take. My eyes strayed further down my body to where I had a full black leg brace on. "What the hell happened to my leg?"

"You shattered your knee. We think that's from hitting the dashboard as you flew out of the vehicle. He fixed that too. I expect the recovery to be slow on both counts, and you might have to have another surgery or two, but you should recover fully."

"Another surgery? How many have I had?"

"Five so far. One on your head and where we reattached your arm enough so that it wouldn't die, then you had another one a few days later to fix everything on your arm, and one on your leg a couple of days later. They did a second surgery on your shoulder about three weeks ago, and a second one on your knee last week."

"Wait? What? How the hell long have I been here?"

The doctor looked at my father and then back at me. "Ethan, you've been in a coma for eleven weeks."

I stared at him and then turned to my father. Were they serious? Eleven weeks? How was that possible?

"You're joking, right?"

"No, at first, we weren't sure if you'd survive at all, but then we put you into a medically induced coma so you could heal. You fought us sometimes, and then you stopped fighting and started healing. We took you off the drugs to keep you in a coma, and you have remained there for seven weeks. We figured that eventually, you'd wake up when you were ready."

I shifted my eyes around the room, unsure how to digest this information.

The doctor patted my arm. "Look, you're awake, and you seem to be doing really well. We want to keep you calm and unstressed if we can so you don't revert into an unconscious state. In the meantime, we are going to start tests, and we can get you scheduled with a therapist to evaluate your neurological functions as well as your physical functions and make a game plan."

"Do you think I'm going to recover enough to go back to work? I'm a police officer."

"Ethan, you survived an accident that I didn't think anyone could survive. I think that if Wes Young hadn't been there at the scene, you wouldn't have lived, but he did a trauma surgery on you in the helicopter on the way here that saved your damn life. If you can survive that accident, you are one tough son of a bitch, and I don't doubt that you will make a full enough recovery to be back on the force as quickly as you can."

"Thanks, Doc."

"You're welcome, Ethan. I'll check in with you again later after a few of your test results come in."

After the doctor left, my sister came around to my other side. "I'm going to go call everyone and let them know they can come to see you."

"No, don't," I told her softly. "Look, I'm glad you two are here, but I don't want to see anyone else, not right now."

"No one?" my father asked.

I shook my head. "No, I need some time to think. I have to process everything that he said and get this testing done. Just let everyone know I'm alright, and I'll give you a call in a day or two. Then you guys can visit."

My sister looked stricken. "Ethan, we have been here every single day watching over you. We can't just walk away now."

I snapped at her, "I appreciate that Cara, but I need some damn space to think. Is that alright with you?"

She shuffled back slightly and peered at my father. "Cara, go wait in the hallway."

She clamped her jaw, and I wasn't sure if that was to keep herself from crying or shouting. She turned and rushed out the door.

"Ethan, that was a little rude. She was worried about you. We all were."

"I'm sorry, I get it, but I have a lot to think about."

"Can I at least let Riley know you are awake? She's been begging to see you."

I stared at my father, my heart aching in a way that had nothing to do with my physical injuries. "No. I do not want to see Riley. I have nothing to say to her right now."

"Ethan, is that wise?"

"Dad, I'm a grown man, and when it comes to her, I don't always make the best decisions, but this one might be the right one. I don't want to see her. She's better off without me."

"Ethan—"

I lifted my hand to stop him and closed my eyes. "I'm tired, Dad. Just go. I love you."

I heard him sigh, and then he kissed my brow and turned and walked out of the room without another word.

After he left, I opened my eyes and stared at the ceiling. I had been here for eleven weeks. That would make Riley about twenty-seven weeks pregnant. How big was she now? Was the baby healthy? Did Riley have problems after the accident? How bad were they?

I frowned. Riley had done her entire pregnancy alone. For twenty-seven weeks, she had done it on her own. I had physically been a part of it for maybe three days. That didn't count our daily video chats, just the time that I was physically with her.

In that time, I had upset her over and over again. I had accused her of things, and I had tried to pressure her into other things. I remembered the party and the proposal, and I remembered what she said to me. She'd told me that she didn't love me, but not just that, she'd said that she couldn't love me.

In that moment that she'd said that, I realized that I would never have her no matter what I did for her. A moment later, I had almost killed myself, her, and our baby.

A tear ran down my cheek as I realized now that I could never be with her. Not because she didn't love me, but because I could never show her how sorry I was for my recklessness. For putting her life on the line, for almost killing our child.

I would step out of her life, give up my rights to my child if that's what made her happy. As another tear ran down my cheek, I knew that it was time to say goodbye to Riley forever.

CHAPTER TWENTY-EIGHT

RILEY

I was out of the hospital five days after the crash and home in bed for another two weeks. My siblings and my parents took turns staying with me to make sure I stayed off my feet. I could use the bathroom, walk from room to room, but nothing else. No lifting, no standing for more than five minutes, no nothing else.

By three weeks out, I was ready to lose my mind and so damn thankful that I was finally allowed to be off bed rest, as long as I took it easy. Next was to get to the hospital and see Ethan.

The problem was, Ethan was still in a coma, and only his family could see him. I'd stopped at the café to speak with Coral shortly after I'd been released from bed rest, but she had been short and distant with me, saying that they didn't even know if he would ever wake up. I felt her anger. She didn't need to say it.

She blamed me.

I blamed myself.

TWO MORE WEEKS WENT BY, and there were no changes in Ethan's condition. Wesley was the one that updated me as he checked in on him while he worked in the hospital.

At first, Wes didn't want to tell me, but I had forced him to, explaining to him that I felt to blame for this and that I deserved to know how bad he was. I was the one to do it to him. No, I hadn't crashed into him, but I had distracted him.

Through all of this, I realized how much Ethan meant to me. I missed him so much that at night, I would lie there and cry. I would tell our daughter stories about him, things that he would laugh about. I'd share things that he liked and didn't. I told her how strong and handsome and caring he was, and how much he loved her—how much he had loved me.

He wouldn't love me anymore now. Not after I had almost cost him his life, might have cost him his job if he couldn't perform as he had. I knew the requirements of being a police officer.

But I realized one other thing as I lay there each night and looked at his picture each day. I loved him. I loved him so much that it hurt. Sometimes the pain would squeeze my heart, and I'd wind up on the floor sobbing at the thought of losing him. Other times, I wanted to laugh at the realization that I did love him.

But was it too late?

I had heard that Ethan was more stable now, but he was still unconscious. No one knew when he would wake up, or if he would. I prayed every day that he would. That somehow, I would have the chance to apologize for everything that I did. I hoped that he would forgive me and love me and that we could do everything that he wanted to do.

Suddenly, the thought of having a family without him wasn't something I wanted. I needed Ethan. Our daughter needed Ethan. Now Ethan needed to come back to us.

✳

A KNOCK CAME at my door eleven weeks and a day after the accident. I had not seen Ethan since that fateful moment of the accident, but I had dreamed of him every night in a million ways.

I opened the door to see Richard standing there, and my knees began to shake immediately. "Is he dead?"

Richard stepped forward, taking me by the shoulders. "He's alive, Riley. He woke up today."

"He did?" I asked as I stared up at his father with watery eyes. Richard touched my cheek and nodded. "How is he?"

I was so afraid to hear that he might have woken up and not known anyone or that maybe he wouldn't even be able to talk. Over the last few weeks, I had been doing a lot of research, and Wes had told me repeatedly to stop being an internet MD.

Richard led me over to the sofa and we sat down. "He was awake and talking. The doctor is putting him through a lot of tests today, but Ethan seems like himself, Riley."

I put my face into my hands and sobbed for a moment while our daughter kicked my stomach as if she were celebrating the news. I rubbed my hand over my belly as I wiped my tears away. "That's great news, Richard. When can I see him?"

His eyes dropped for a moment. "Right now, he's dealing with a lot and trying to digest some things. He said that he doesn't want to see anyone for a few days."

"Not even me?"

He shook his head. "Not even you, but he's glad you and the baby are alright."

I gnawed on my bottom lip. What must be going through his mind. "Richard, I have to see him as soon as I can. He thinks that I don't love him. I told him that I didn't, but I was so wrong! I don't want a life without your son in it. You know that."

He gave me a sad smile. "I know that, Riley. I know. That's why I want to give him twenty-four hours, and then tomorrow, I want to take you to see him. I think it would be good for him to see you."

"Thank you." I clasped his weathered hand in mine. "Thank you so much, Richard."

That night, I did a lot of thinking about what I was going to say, and by the time Richard picked me up, I had a good idea. I was a nervous wreck but excited too, and the baby was bouncing around in my belly like she was doing flips.

At the hospital, Richard left me in the waiting room. He had to speak to Ethan first and get permission to bring me back. It took him about twenty minutes before he returned, a smile on his face. "He wants to see you. Go on back through those doors, and he's in the third room."

Richard patted my shoulder as I passed him, and I walked slowly toward the doors. If I had stopped, I think my knees would have started knocking against one another. I pushed the button to enter the unit and then glanced back at Richard, who nodded.

I paused outside the door to his room, my hand on my extended belly, my heart in my throat, and then I stepped into his room. He turned his face toward me. His eyes drifted down my face to my stomach, where they stayed for a moment.

I stepped closer to the bed, taking in every detail of him. His hair was way too long on one side but really short on the other from where it had been shaved to repair his skull. His beard needed a trim. He liked a little scruff, but it was too long for his taste. His color was pale, and his eyes were watchful.

I wanted to fall to my knees as I stared into his blue eyes. I hadn't realized how much I missed them until I saw them again. "Ethan," I breathed the word as I stopped beside his bed and reached for his hand.

He held it for a moment, even squeezed it momentarily before he let it go and laid his hand over his chest away from me. "Riley."

"How are you doing?"

He blinked once, then twice. "You don't really care, so it doesn't matter. I'll make this short and sweet because I'm tired and it's been a long day. I appreciate you coming, but I don't want you here."

"Ethan—"

He put his hand up. "I need to say this, Riley. You told me how you felt, and I was stupid to believe that I could change your mind. I almost killed you and the baby, and for that, I'm sorry. I'll stay out of your life now. In fact, I'll sign over my rights to the baby if that's what you want."

My jaw dropped. Ethan not only didn't want me, but he didn't want our daughter? "Ethan, you can't mean that. We need you."

"No, you don't."

"We do!" I reached for his hand again and clung to it when he tried to pull it back. "Ethan, I was wrong to say what I did. Not because I shouldn't have said it, but because it wasn't the truth. I love you! I need you! Our daughter needs you!"

Ethan's eyes widened as I mentioned it was a girl, and then he tugged his hand back. "You don't need me, and you two would be better off without me." He turned his face away from me, and tears streaked my face.

"Ethan, you can't mean that! I love you!"

"Go, Riley, and don't come back."

"Ethan!" I begged him, but a nurse came in and started dragging me out of the room. "Ethan, this is not over! I love you, damn it! I will prove to you that I do!"

As I was pulled around the corner, I saw him still staring away, but I could have sworn I saw moisture on his cheeks. How could he do this? How could he not only not want me, but not want our daughter?

The nurse led me to the outer door and then left me standing there crying, one hand on my belly, the other on my forehead as I leaned against the wall. Strong arms wrapped around me. "What happened?"

"He doesn't want me. He doesn't want our daughter."

"Oh, Riley, he doesn't mean that. He's upset. He blames himself for the accident. I know he does. Come on, let's get you home. I'll talk to him."

I sucked up the pain and the tears until I was home, and after Richard left, I curled up in bed and cried myself to sleep. I apologized over and over again to our daughter for how I had screwed everything up.

TWO WEEKS LATER, Ethan was released from the hospital and sent to a rehab facility where he stayed for almost six weeks.

It was the day of my baby shower when I learned that he had come home two days earlier on January sixth. Charlotte had told me. None of his sisters were here for the shower, and none of them would speak to me.

I'd run into Candy one day at the store, and she had seemed nervous to see me. She'd been pleasant enough, but she had rushed away as quickly as she could. Only Richard checked in on me and sent his love every few days.

He came for tea just the other day and told me that he'd tried to talk to Ethan again, but he was stubborn about his decision. He truly felt that our daughter and I would be better off without him.

I knew he was wrong, and after a lot of talking with Charlotte, Roxy, and Dani, I'd concluded that he ultimately blamed himself for the accident. He thought that he had almost killed us because of something that he had done, and not because I had distracted him with my words.

If I was truthful with myself, the blame was to be put on both of us, but that crash had been a wake-up call for me. If it hadn't happened, I might not have realized how much I loved the man. How much I needed him in my life. Not just for our daughter, but for me. Now I had a couple of weeks to get him to listen to me, and we could get this fixed before the baby was born.

I had already decided that I would not have this baby without him at my side. I was thinking about that as I came down the stairs from putting something in the nursery. A loud bang from the kitchen startled me, and I stepped wrong, losing my footing and falling down the last three steps on my butt.

Holy crap! My back! I sat there as Roxy ran around the corner of the kitchen. "Riley! Are you alright?"

"Yeah, I just slipped down those last few steps. I think I bruised my tailbone. Help me get up."

Roxy and Dani rushed to help me off the floor. As soon as I stood, a sharp pain went through my stomach, and a gush of fluid ran down my legs.

"Shit! My water just broke!" I said as I stared at them.

Roxy looked down and began to speak as I screamed in pain and almost dropped to my knees. "Oh, shit! That's not just your fluid, Ry. You're bleeding!"

"I'll call 9-1-1," Charlotte yelled down the hallway as they put me back to the floor.

I grabbed Roxy's arm. "Get Ethan! Please bring him to the hospital! I can't have this baby without him there! Please, Roxy!"

"I will. I'll go as soon as the ambulance gets here."

"No! Go now! Go, drag him if you have to!"

Roxy rushed away, and a few minutes later, I heard the door

close. The pains kept coming, and Dani and Charlotte stayed by my side until the ambulance arrived. Luckily, my brother wasn't the paramedic, and a few minutes later, we were on the way to the hospital. Charlotte was holding my hand, Dani following us, and the whole way, I prayed that Ethan would get the stick out of his ass and arrive in time.

CHAPTER TWENTY-NINE

ETHAN

Other than my father and Carmen, no one mentioned Riley to me. My father made sure to bring her name up every time he was around, and I got tired of telling him that I didn't want to hear about it.

After he'd brought her to the hospital, he'd taken her home and then driven all the way back to the hospital to ream me out. He had gone on and on about how I was the most stubborn person he had ever met and how I was throwing my life away. He told me I had disappointed him, and I didn't bother to tell him I was disappointed in myself. I let him go on and on, pretending to listen, but in actuality, I let most of the words float in one ear and right out the other.

By the time I got into the rehab facility, I had figured out how to block out thoughts of Riley altogether. As soon as I was well enough, I was going to sell my house and move closer to work. Even though I had a long road ahead, I knew that I would recover enough to do my job. I might have a little problem with my knee once in a while, but my mind was still sharp and intact. If I were farther away, I wouldn't run the chance of running into her or the baby.

The baby was where I got hung up. I knew that I would eventually get over Riley, but how could I get over not being with my daughter? Perhaps I hadn't thought that part out fully. Except, yeah, I had.

I had almost killed the woman I loved and my child before she—it was a girl—even took her first breath. What kind of a father would I be if I couldn't even protect her while she was safely tucked inside her mother?

I was a cop, for god's sake, and my life was in jeopardy every time I put my badge on. I couldn't do that to my child or the woman I loved. I couldn't and I wouldn't.

I had missed Christmas at home, but was thankfully released in early January. Instead of heading straight home, I was taken to my father's for another week. They wanted to make sure that I could manage okay before being on my own. I didn't mind it that much, except he had to bring up Riley's name just about every freaking hour.

Today had been even more brutal because as he cooked lunch, he went on and on about how many things he'd gotten for the baby for the shower. He described the clothing down to the little snaps and the bags of diapers and the monitor system that he'd purchased.

I hated him for telling me all this, but I hated myself more because I hadn't been a part of it. For the next eighteen years, this was what was going to happen. I'd hear all about the child's life but not be involved. Maybe I needed to move farther than forty-five minutes away.

I had a feeling that no distance would be far enough to stop the pain. We had just finished our late lunch, and I was using my cane to walk into the living room when I heard a car pull into the driveway and start honking its horn. I glanced out the window and saw Roxy jumping out of her car and running toward the door. Something wasn't right, and my father passed me and went to open the door.

"Roxy, what's wrong?" he asked as he pulled open the door and a cold blast of January air slammed into me.

She looked between me and my father. "It's Riley. She fell down the stairs. They are rushing her to the hospital."

My leg began to buckle, and I sat down quickly before I fell. The urge to go to her was so strong, but she wasn't mine to go to.

"Ethan, get your coat," my father snapped at me, and I shook my head.

"I'm not going."

"Oh, the hell you aren't. Your baby and her momma are in the hospital and need you. You need to stop feeling sorry for yourself and get moving."

Roxy stepped forward nervously. "Ethan, Riley told me to come get you. She needs you. She said she is not having this baby without you."

I laughed. "Yeah, I'd like to see her hold that progression back."

"Ethan Michael Winston, you get off your ass right now and get your coat."

"Dad, I told you that I don't want anything to do with Riley or the baby."

"Why?" Roxy asked. "Why, Ethan? When you hit your head, did you forget how much you loved them? Did you forget that just minutes before that, you had vowed to be there for them through everything? I sure didn't. Your father didn't, and Riley sure as hell didn't."

"Roxy, I almost killed her and the baby. I said I'd keep them safe, and the first thing I did was upset Riley and almost kill them both!" I yelled at her, and she came closer, getting down on her knees in front of me.

"Ethan, that was an accident. You were both upset. The blame falls on both of you for even getting in the damn car in the first place! You should have stood in the front yard and screamed at one another until you worked it out and fell into each other's arms again. Because you always do."

She put her hand over my knee. "When you almost died, Riley changed. She realized suddenly just how much you meant to her, how much you do mean to her. She needs you, Ethan. That little girl is going to need her father, and Riley loves you so damn much."

"No, she doesn't. She told me that day that she didn't love me."

"She said that because she was afraid, Ethan. She was scared to death and freaking out at your proposal in front of everyone. If you had given her time, she would have come around. When you almost died, she realized how stupid she had been, how wrong about so many things. The day she came to the hospital to see you, she was coming to apologize to you and ask for your forgiveness."

"She doesn't need my forgiveness," I stated.

"Then show her that," my father growled. "Now get your damn coat. You are going to get your ass to the hospital. You are going to tell that woman that you love her and that the baby that she is carrying is the most important thing in your life. You got that, Ethan? Because if you don't, I'm going to drop-kick your ass right into the street and hope that you land on your head again to knock some damn sense into you."

I actually started to laugh because I could see my father doing just that. I began to get up, and Roxy jumped to her feet and helped me.

"Ethan, you ride with Roxy. I'll meet you all down there after I make a few phone calls."

"Who are you calling?"

"Your sisters," he stated. "It's about time this stupid little guilt trip is over, and you all start acting like the human beings your momma and I raised. Now go!"

"Pop," I called before he walked out of the room. I walked over to him and paused. "Thanks."

He slapped my arm. "Get out of here."

I took my time going down the front steps because there was a little ice on them, and then Roxy and I hurried to her car. She drove way slower than I would have liked, but the last thing we needed was another accident.

The whole way there, Roxy talked about the things that Riley had been doing to prepare for the baby's birth. Not as in decorating, but as in how she would sit and tell the baby stories about me and play my favorite music.

By the time we got to the hospital, I was ready to fall to pieces. Did Riley really love me? Could I make this work? Could I be a good father and possibly a husband to her?

In the waiting room, we found Charlotte and Daniella. "They are doing a few tests on her right now. I already called everyone," Charlotte said.

Just after she said that a nurse came out and called Charlotte's name. "You're here for Riley Young?"

"Yes, we are."

"They are rushing her up to surgery; her placenta is rupturing, and they will need to do an emergency C-section." Roxy clung to Charlotte with a gasp. The nurse turned to me. "Are you Ethan?"

I nodded, surprised that she would ask.

"Okay, you can come with me. She wants you in the delivery room."

"What?" I asked as the nurse started to walk away.

Roxy pushed me. "Go, Ethan! Go tell her that you love her and watch your baby girl being born."

I stared at her but then hurried after the nurse. Riley really did want me at her side, and holy crap! I was about to become a father. I walked as fast as I could with my cane, and the nurse brought me to an elevator.

"Take this up to the third floor, and the nurse at the station will direct you from there."

A moment later, the elevator was going up, and I was trying not to freak out. The doors opened on the third floor, and I stepped out to a desk a few feet away. "I'm Ethan Winston. Riley Young was just brought up here. She's my—she's giving birth to my daughter."

"Ethan, go right down that hall to the locker room and change into a set of scrubs. There will be a shelf right inside. Just grab a bag, and it will have everything that you need. They are prepping her. I'll let them know you are coming."

Just then, I heard my name being screamed from down the hall.

The nurse laughed. "Yeah, she's been doing that since she got up here. Hurry up so she'll calm down."

I practically ran to the locker room and pulled the first bag off the shelf to start changing. I shoved my stuff into a locker and tried to open the door with shaking hands. I paused in the hallway, unsure of what to do, but then I heard my name screamed again, and I followed the sound.

A nurse stopped me at the door. "I assume you're Ethan?" she asked with a hopeful look in her eye.

"Yeah."

"Okay, the cane will need to be left here, but there is a stool you can sit on. Come on." I gave her my cane, where she set it aside and then took her arm in case I needed balance as she took me into the cold room. It was scary as hell in there for me, and I couldn't imagine what it would be like for her.

The minute she saw me, she started crying. "Ethan, you made it."

The nurse let go of me as we reached her side, and I leaned over her, my eyes filling with tears. "Oh, baby. I'm so sorry. I'm here."

I kissed Riley, then leaned my forehead against her as the love and emotion poured out of me and our tears mixed.

"Thank god you are here, Ethan. I'm Doctor Rutherford. Can we do the delivery now, please?"

"Yes, sir," I said to him as I took the chair next to Riley. I peered around the curtain and saw her huge belly jutting up from the center of a sea of blue dressings. The doctor put a scalpel to her stomach, and I quickly looked away. I wasn't ready to watch that shit!

Instead, I stared at Riley. "I'm so sorry, Ry."

"Hush, the only thing you have to apologize for is not being around to put all the baby stuff together."

I chuckled as I wiped a tear from her face.

"I love you, Ethan. I love you more than I could have ever imagined loving someone. When I thought you might die, I wanted to curl up in bed with you and go with you. I couldn't imagine a world without you in it with our baby."

"I'm here, Riley. I'm here as long as you want me, baby."

"Marry me, Ethan," Riley said in a rush. "Please!"

"Figures you'd ask me." I chuckled. "Yes, I'll marry you, baby."

"Ethan?" I lifted my head to the doctor as he called my name. He glanced my way. "If you want to see your child being born, stand up and look over the curtain now."

I glanced at Riley, and she nodded. I stood as I held her hand in mine and watched as the doctor pulled a tiny human out of Riley's belly. He held the baby up for only a second for me to see, and then someone took the baby from him, and he handed me a pair of scissors.

"Do you want to do the honors?"

I nodded and took them from his hand, reaching over the curtain to snip the cord. A few moments later, there was a wail on the side of the room, and I looked down at Riley as she started to laugh and cry at the same time.

"We have a baby girl," she said as I leaned forward to kiss her.

I smiled through my tears. "We have a baby girl."

CHAPTER THIRTY

RILEY

I wasn't sure that Ethan would make it, and I swore that they were not going to do this surgery before he arrived. When I got word that he was here, my tension eased, but I still wouldn't let them start until he was seated beside me.

To see him as emotional as I was told me that I had made the right decision. This was where our future needed to start. It needed to begin at the moment our daughter took her first breath in this world.

While both of us might blame ourselves, and maybe the other, a little bit for the accident, I knew that we would make it past that. Ethan and I had come too far not to.

I had every intention of being his wife and of building our family into something as special as what my parents and his parents had. I owed it to him. I owed it to myself.

It was funny how we learn things about ourselves and realize what we know about others. It was hours later after our families had come and seen the baby and wished us well when I lay back in bed and watched him stare down at our daughter, Corey. He was touching her little fingers as her other hand was curled under her chin.

"She sleeps like you. A hand tucked under her chin."

I laughed. "I can't wait to see how she is like you."

"What do you mean?"

I smiled at him. "I mean, is she going to like whole wheat bagels and turkey bacon better than plain and real bacon? Or will she hang up her sweatpants as you do, instead of putting them in a drawer as most people do?"

He smirked at me, but I wasn't done yet. "I wonder if she'll eat all of her veggies before she eats her meat and potatoes or if she'll like any kind of hot dog or be partial to only all-beef ones like you."

He chuckled, and I continued. "I also wonder if she will like green as much as you do and if she'll want a matching Flyers jersey so she can watch the games with you."

He grinned. "See, you do know things about me."

"Yeah, like a million little things," I replied. "Over the last few weeks, I've been writing them all down and sharing them with Corey."

"You have, huh?"

"Yeah. I wanted her to know as much about her father as she could."

He stood and came to sit on the edge of the bed, his face a little sad. "I'm sorry that I missed it all, Riley. I really screwed up."

"Well, I guess we will just have to do it all over again."

He hiked a brow, and I put my hand up. "I mean, in a few years. I'm not sure I'm ready for that again quite yet."

"You want to have another child with me?"

I reached up and touched his face. "I want to have three children with you, Ethan, and I want to grow old in your arms."

"Well, how about before we have another kid, we just practice the art of making them—a lot."

"Oh, I like that idea."

He leaned forward, kissing me tenderly, and then stared

down at me as he whispered, "You two are my everything, and I am going to do everything in my power to protect you and love you the best that I can."

"That's all we ask of you." I smiled as I cupped his cheek. "That's all we need from you."

THE END

LOVING A YOUNG SERIES

If you enjoyed Riley, consider leaving a quick review! The best way to compliment an author is to leave a few words for them in a review.

Leave your review here: Riley

The Loving a Young Series consists of six books involving the Young Siblings: Wesley, Henley, Huntley, Bradley, Riley and Kayley.

Wesley, Book 1
An overprotective mother, an injured child, and a handsome doctor. Can an accident create a family?

Charlotte Bennett is not a fan of strangers. She reacts without listening when she sees a man touching her daughter at the park. It's only later when her daughter is rushed to the hospital, that Charlotte realizes how wrong she had been to accuse the stranger of inappropriate behavior.

Doctor Wesley Young only wanted to help the tender-aged girl he witnessed fall, but when her mother attacks him at the park, he's left stunned. When little Marisol arrives in the emergency department, the mother makes more of an impression on him than the cut she left on his face.

Things heat up quickly when Marisol is no longer Wes's patient, but when traumatic things from Charlotte's past are revealed, Wes isn't sure that Charlotte is the woman for him. Can Charlotte find a way to explain it all so that Wes will accept both her and her daughter?

Henley, Book 2
Ever the optimist, Roxy is excited about the future, but when she finds out about the sexy Paramedic's past, can you get over it?

Being a wedding planner is hard, especially when someone always tries to steal your business, and your family doesn't support you. However, Roxanne Novak is determined to keep her business afloat—no matter what. When Roxy is in a car accident hurrying to meet a potential bride, she's injured and scared, but paramedic Henley Young takes excellent care of her.

Henley loves his job and thrives on the adrenaline of helping people in need. Maybe that's why when he meets Roxy, he's inclined to help her with more than just medical care. Hooking her up with his older brother Wesley and his bride-to-be could be just what she needs. It might also be the start of something between Henley and the spunky little wedding planner.

With a surprise job offer Roxy, she finds herself rethinking her entire business plan. Excited at the prospect and another chance, Roxy and Henley begin making plans. After Roxy accidentally learns of Henley's past relationship, everything she knew about him is questioned.

Can Roxy and Henley put the past to bed and move forward to something that might be more than what either had ever hoped for?

Huntley, Book 3
When Daniella's life is threatened again, can she pull herself out of her fictional world long enough to see the truth?

Daniella Knight works hard to create suspenseful and romantic tales, but she shutters herself from the world after a violent interaction with a fan. When her house catches on fire, she and her protection dog, Tigger, are forced to rely on the help of strangers.

Huntley Young loves being in the thick of the action—especially if that action has something to do with his job as a firefighter. When Huntley stops the homeowner from returning inside the house, he has no clue that he just placed himself firmly in the hero department of her latest book.

As Hunt and Daniella get to know each other, Daniella's creative mind sometimes has trouble separating reality and fiction. When danger strikes again, will Daniella be able to see what is right in front of her, or will her past trauma protect her while hiding inside her romantic fictional world?

Riley, Book 4
Will Riley finally admit that she's in love with Ethan, or will she lose him forever?

Riley is always the life of the party, and Ethan is there to pick her up and keep her together. He knows her almost as well as she knows herself, and he knows she will never love him as he does her.

Now Ethan wants more out of life and love, but Riley continues to deny her feelings and insists they are only friends with benefits. When a training opportunity comes up that will get Ethan out of town for months, he jumps on it—finally, a way to get over Riley and move on.

With Ethan gone and a new guy in her life, Riley deals with several emotional issues without the help of her best friend. A family emergency has Ethan feeling lost without Riley to lean on, but he refuses to go to her and seeks solace with another.

Will Riley make the right choices and finally admit how she feels, or will she find herself alone and falling further down the rabbit hole?

Kayley, Book 5
When Kayley falls for a younger man, can she learn to accept her feelings, or will she lose something she didn't even know she wanted?

Kayley Young's life is about to undergo a few profound changes. Independent Kayley Young is a real estate agent in New York and loves her life as a single woman. She's not one to get tied down and leaves the baby-making to her siblings.

Officer Cameron Sexton is new on the job, a veteran of the military, and proud of his dedication to the job. Unfortunately, he finds himself annoyed at his lackadaisical sergeant, who should hang up his gun belt before getting someone hurt. When Cameron is dispatched to a burglary, he meets Kayley Young and is instantly attracted to her. Cameron has a feeling she reciprocates those feelings, except she's a little leery that he is ten years younger than her.

When Kayley's life starts taking a turn for the worst, she depends more on the attractive young man she has let into her bed for fun than she intended. Her original thought of enjoying the moment starts to last longer, but Kayley's not sure that dating a man ten years her junior is wise for the long haul. Especially with the rest of the changes that have happened in her life. Can Kayley come to terms with the age difference, or will her family sway her away from the younger man?

Bradley, Book 6
Bradley is set in his ways, but when his sister asks for him to help her friend, he finds more than he bargained for.

Bradley Young is the eldest sibling of the Young family and the only one previously married. After losing his wife to cancer, he's used to caring for his two kids alone. The thought of dating is not something he's interested in, not with a busy construction business and a family that always needs help.

Nolan Nickels needed a change, and with the help of her good friend, Kayley, she left New York and came to Millerstown to take a teaching position at the middle school. She has always been a tomboy and loves to fix things with her hands and play sports.

With a new house in her name, Nolan seeks out the perfect plan to get the house ready so she can bring her two daughters home, but is her fixer-upper more than she bargained for?

When Kayley finally gets Brad to stop by the house to check

something, Brad finds himself more than intrigued with the spitfire, Nolan. Will he finally find the woman to spend his life with, or will she halt on any future?

If you loved the Young's, make sure to join the Winston's as the rest of them fine their forever love.

The *Loving a Winston Series* is a five-book, steamy adult romance series spins off the six-book *Loving a Young Series*. Characters from both series will appear from book to book. Each book is a standalone romance with bits of suspense.

The Loving a Winston Series
Cara - Evan - Candy - Carmen - Coral

The *Loving a Lancaster Series* will begin publishing in 2025 and spins off the *Loving a Winston Series*. This series is anticipated to be at least eight books long.

LOVING A WINSTON SERIES

The *Loving a Winston Series* is a five-book steamy romance series that spins off of the *Loving a Young Series*. Characters from both series will appear from book to book. Each book is a standalone romance with suspense and spicy romance scenes.

Cara, Book 1

What happens when the man you fall for is all wrong for you?

Cara Winston has always been a bit of a rebel and an adrenaline junkie. As a helicopter pilot and paramedic, she relies on that to do her job.

When Cara and her team respond to a multi-vehicle accident involving motorcycles, she's expecting the worst. What she's not expecting is to find herself intrigued by the blue eyes of a man wearing motorcycle gang colors.

Ryan Vigilante rides the road, mostly on two wheels, not

four. When several of his club end up in an accident on the highway, Ryan never expects to see a future in the eyes of the intense female paramedic. The only problem is, she's way out of his league, and he knows that getting involved with her could only put her in jeopardy.

With Cara's family trying to keep them apart and Ryan's club breaking the law, Cara finds herself more of a rebel than usual. Will things work out for Cara and Ryan, or will Cara's law enforcement brother, Ethan, find a way to put a stop to it for good?

Evan, Book 2

What happens when she's not really who you think she is?

EVAN WINSTON IS DEDICATED to his job as a registered nurse in the ICU department of the local hospital. He's one hundred percent focused on the needs of his patients and his family, or at least he usually is. That all changes the day a woman visits one of his patients and turns his world upside down.

Laney Marshall wants nothing more than to help people who struggle. Especially those women and children who are fighting to survive domestic violence situations. After losing someone close to her to an abusive man, she is determined to do everything in her power to help.

Unfortunately, Laney has people that don't want her to do that. In fact, they don't even want her in this town or even the state of Pennsylvania. They prefer her on the other side of the country, where they think she belongs, living the life planned for her.

Can Laney and Evan find a way to build a relationship while keeping others from getting involved, or will the revealed secrets be enough to end any chance of a future before it begins?

Candy, Book 3

What happens when your lustful heart wins over your intellectual mind?

WHEN CANDY'S SISTER, Cara, was dating outlaw biker member Ryan Vigilante, Candy paid little attention to Ryan's club buddy, Bollard. Sure, Bollard, who works behind the bar at the local tavern, was pleasing on the eyes and made a mean chocolate martini, but he was an outlaw, and that's not the kind of person Candy associates with.

Michael Bollard is out of the club now, and he hopes to purchase the tavern. He had never wanted anything more than his bikes and the club, but now, Mike has hopes of building a future, a future that is colliding with sexy and intelligent Candy Winston in ways he could have never imagined.

Just when he thinks he might have his future figured out, a stranger enters the bar with a surprise he never saw coming. Will that surprise send Candy running for higher ground, or will it cement her future in the tavern with Mike?

Carmen, Book 4

What happens when your first love returns to town—twenty years later?

CHILD PSYCHOLOGIST, Carmen Winston, spends a lot of time at the schools, and when she come across a man and the name of a new student, she is thrown back to a time of young love and dreamy hopes of the perfect future.

Tim Kohl lived in Millerstown for six years before his parents moved him across the country. He never expected to return, and when he does, it's with three kids in tow. The last thing he expects to find in town is his high school sweetheart still beautiful as ever and single.

When sparks fly, can these two put the past behind them and plan a future, or will the years apart separate them before they can figure it out.

Coral, Book 5

What happens you overhear your family talking to the man you've fallen for?

CORAL WINSTON HAS FELT out of touch with her family since her mother passed away and throws everything she has into her coffee café. When her family forces her to take a vacation, they all decide to come along for the fun.

Landan Lancaster is the oldest of the eight Lancaster children, and he's still trying to deal with walking away from his cheating bride the night before their wedding many months prior. When a large family comes to stay in the Lancaster guest house on the lake, he finds himself intrigued by the woman standing at the water's edge.

On the slopes, Landan realizes he has met his match in more ways than one, and Coral begins to feel as if she has finally found where she belongs. When a conversation is overheard, Coral gets the wrong idea and flees, only to find a mountain of trouble waiting for her back home.

Can Coral overcome the issues facing her and find her way

back to the beautiful mountains and water of Lake Tahoe, or will Landan lose her before he can ever call her his own?

COMING IN 2025
Loving the Lancasters! Another 8 book Spin-off to keep the reading pleasure coming!

LOVING A LANCASTER SERIES

The Loving a Lancaster Series spins off of the Loving a Winston Series. In Coral's book, you are introduced to the Lancaster family while she is on vacation in Lake Tahoe. This series will consist of seven books, and stared with Leo.

Leo - Book 1

Leo Lancaster is coming home to Lake Tahoe. As a successful stockbroker and business owner, Leo has decided to open another office in Truckee and work out of that one instead of his Vegas office. Now, he must locate a house and get himself settled, and the last thing he expects to find on his return is love.

Heather McClain is a devoted mother of two teens, and a widow from Ohio. When her best friend encourages her to go on a girls trip to Lake Tahoe, she decides to take a break from the chaos at home and try to have fun. Only their antics are more than Heather bargained for.

Lucky for her, Leo is around to rescue her and the two of them quickly grow close, but is Heather ready to let go of her husband's memory and move forward into a relationship, or more importantly, are her children prepared to accept a new man into their mother's life when she surprises them with a trip to the lake?

Luna - Book 2

WHILE LUNA LANCASTER loves Lake Tahoe, she thrives in the outdoors near her home in Sedona, Arizona. When Luna's good friend, Sadie, plans a visit and decides to bring a guest, Luna is excited to show them the sights of the beautiful Red Rocks around her home.

Unfortunately, Luna's friend can't make it at the last minute, and Luna finds herself entertaining Trace Hampton alone. The chemistry between them sparks the moment they meet. The problem is that Luna thinks Trace and Sadie are a couple, and she does everything possible to hide her feelings and not act on them.

When Trace reveals that he is not involved with Sadie, Luna jumps at the chance to see what they could have, but when Sadie finds out, she's heartbroken that Luna stole the man she likes out from under her.

Will Luna save the friendship and lose the chance at a happily ever after with Trace?

Still to come: Lance, Lily, Laney, Lucas and Levi.

SNEAK PEEK: KAYLEY

Enjoy the first chapter of Kayley, Loving a Young Series, Book 5

Kayley

"*N*ot again!" I groaned as I stood in the entryway to the house. I pulled out my phone and dialed 9-1-1, glancing around as far as I could see as I waited for someone to answer. I knew better than to go any farther into the house. I'd gotten a lecture the last time this had happened. It was last weekend, but a different house on the other side of town.

"9-1-1, what's your emergency?"

"Hi, I'd like to report a burglary."

"A burglary? Is this a home or business?"

"A home."

"And the address?"

"1654 Evergreen Street," I replied.

"And your name?"

"Kayley Young."

"Kayley, are you the homeowner?"

"No, I'm the real estate agent. I have an open house scheduled here for today."

"Are you inside the house?"

"Yes, sort of."

"Have you checked the interior of the residence?"

"No, I learned not to do that after the first one."

"First one?"

"Yeah, another house I have listed had this happen a week ago. The sergeant told me never to step foot into a house that looks like it's been burglarized because you don't know if the suspects are still inside."

"Okay, let me get an officer dispatched. Can you hold on for a moment?"

"Sure," I replied, and I heard her side of the line click. A couple of moments later, she was back.

"Alright, officers are on their way. If you could remain outside, they will check the residence when they arrive to make sure it is safe for you to enter."

"Alright, thank you," I said as I turned and stepped back out the front door. I went to stand by my car, dialing my partner's number as I did.

"Morning, Kayley," Fran said in a deep voice. "Good news already? Did you sell the house to the first person?"

"Sorry to say I have no good news, and I won't have any today. Someone broke into the house and trashed it, just like the other one."

"What?" His deep voice grew louder. "Are you serious?"

"Yes, I am." I sighed as I stared back at the house. Francis McDugal and I had started the real estate agency, McDugal and Young, four years ago. He was a great guy, and I enjoyed working with him. We'd had a brief affair many years ago when we'd first met in Albany, but we had quickly realized that we were much better business partners and friends than lovers. Besides, he was raising a child, and that was a no for me.

Our friendship was easy and predictable. Now we talked about everything together and shared the majority of the workload. Our company had grown so much in the last year that we'd just hired two junior real estate agents to help us. The business and life were good.

The only bad part about our business was that it was so far away from home. When I had moved to New York ten years ago, I'd been hell-bent on leaving the small town behind. I had moved near Albany, and then a few years later, relocated closer to Fran once he'd asked me to start the business with him. Now I was back to living in a small town, which made me miss home —bad, especially after what happened last summer when the Winstons lost their mother so quickly to cancer. I often thought of my parents and checked in with them probably more often than most thirty-eight-year-old women did, but I didn't care.

Maybe it was strange for some people to do that, but it was not with our family. Being one of six children, we were all very close, and we talked often. I made the four-hour drive home when I could, although not as often as I wished. In fact, I had wanted to go home this weekend, but the homeowners begged me to move the open house up. They really had to get out from under this mortgage as they already had a new home and couldn't afford two mortgage payments.

Wait till I told them about this.

"How much damage is there, Kay?"

I huffed, "I don't know. I walked in the front door, saw the entrance light smashed to pieces, and I could see spray paint on the wall in the living room. I called the police and came back outside."

"Jesus, stupid kids! Man, they need another hobby."

"Tell me about it." I sure hoped that the homeowners still

had insurance on this house. "Anyway, I'll wait until the cops finish here, and then I'll call the Beckers and let them know what's going on. Since they live in Detroit now, I'll have to coordinate with the insurance company to get it all fixed. What a pain in the ass!"

"You could get Tina to take care of that for you."

"I might have to, but we did load Tina and Walt with a lot of stuff, didn't we?" I grinned.

He chuckled. "I know. Now I look at all of that and go, how the hell did we stay on top of it?"

"Right? We ran around like chickens with our heads cut off," I told him with a laugh, and a police car turned the corner onto the street, and then a second one. "I gotta go, Fran. The police are pulling up."

"Okay, keep me updated and send me some pictures when you can."

"I will, bye." I hung up as the cars pulled to the curb. When I saw the cop in the second car, I groaned to myself. Sergeant Gerczak was a grumbling old coot who needed to retire.

He was the one who had taken the report last week, and he barely took any information on it. His attitude was, the homeowner's insurance will pay for it, and it's not worth processing the scene for a few hundred dollars' worth of damage. It turned out that a few hundred dollars' worth of damage was over eleven thousand dollars' worth.

I wanted to file a complaint at the station against the sergeant, but Fran had talked me out of it. He said it wasn't worth the aggravation. The insurance company took care of everything, and just last night, we had an offer put down on that house. That's where Fran was right now, at the office dealing with the paperwork to lock down that sale.

My gaze went to the other officer as he climbed out of his car. He was much younger, and I was delighted about that. Sergeant Gerczak hadn't gotten out of his car yet, but the other officer approached me immediately. "Ms. Young? Hi, I'm Officer Sexton. You called about a burglary?"

"Yes, I'm a real estate agent, and I have an open house here today. I stepped in and found damage in the entranceway and called the police."

Sergeant Gerczak joined us. "It's you again. Did you go in and walk around this time?"

Officer Sexton glanced at him and then back to me. "Hello again, Sergeant, and no. I followed your advice and stepped out as soon as I saw the mess."

"Same thing as last time?" he asked gruffly as he looked at the house. His gray hair was matted on one side like it had been resting on something for a while. I wouldn't put it past him that he'd been parked someplace taking a nap. He was old enough to need one.

"I don't know if it's the same since I heeded your warning about checking the residence alone."

He smirked. "Good girl."

I pursed my lips. I was far from being a girl. Officer Sexton spoke up. "It's a good thing you waited outside. We'll go check the residence, and let you know when it's safe to enter."

"Thank you, Officer Sexton." I smiled at him, and he returned it. He had a rather handsome smile, but I couldn't see his eyes because they were hidden behind heavily tinted glasses. His dark hair looked thick and had a wave to it, and he was tall and trim, although his uniform made him look wider.

He stepped around me, and I heard the sergeant murmuring to him as they approached the house. "Just take a report, and let's go. I'm hungry and want to get lunch soon."

I growled under my breath as I crossed my arms over my chest. If this got pushed off as the last one did, I *was* going to file a complaint. In fact, I would do it as soon as I left here today. I wouldn't even tell Fran that I was doing it. Then he couldn't talk me out of it.

I paced as I waited out front, and a few minutes later, Sgt. Gerczak came out. "You can go in. Officer Sexy will handle your report."

Officer Sexy? How unprofessional of him! "Thank you," I managed to say. My parents had taught me manners. Obviously, his hadn't, or he was too old to remember how to use them.

I was staring down at my phone as I approached the front door and slammed into Officer Sexton as he stepped over the threshold. His hands grabbed on to my arms to steady me as we bounced off one another.

"I'm so sorry," he said. "I was looking over my shoulder."

I stared up at him and found myself rather intrigued by his light-green eyes. His dark sunglasses were now perched on top of his head. His eyes were sort of hazel but mostly light green—almost like the seafoam on the Jersey Shore.

"You're not the only one to blame. I was looking at my phone." I took a step back, and his hands dropped from my arms.

"Are you okay?"

"Yes, why wouldn't I be?"

He patted his chest and smiled. "I can't imagine slamming into this hard thing and all my accouterments was very pleasant."

I liked his smile. "Oh, I've slammed into worse," I told him with a chuckle. "You ever fall off a horse into a briar patch before?"

His grin went lopsided. "No, that one I have not done."

"Yeah, well, slamming into the dirt is a little more uncomfortable than your body, and a briar patch causes all kinds of other issues," I replied dryly.

"I'm going to take your word for it, Ms. Young." He stepped to the side. "Come on in, and we can go over the damage together. There is a lot."

"I figured." I huffed as I stepped past him into the living room and brought up my camera on the phone.

"Where are the homeowners?" he asked.

"The Beckers live in Detroit, or near it anyway. He got transferred out there last month."

"Can you give me a moment? I want to go grab my notebook out of my patrol car so that I can write details down on this as we go through the house."

I spiked a brow. "You're going to do more than just take my name and phone number?"

He looked confused. "Um, yeah. I need to take a full report. I know you said you have an open house today, but this will take a little while. I also want to dust a few places for prints."

"Dust for prints?" Oh, could I be so lucky to have someone who was going to take their job seriously? Yippie!

He laughed like he was uncomfortable. "Yeah, that's kind of what we do when there is a burglary."

"Well, thank you!" I said quickly. "I—" I paused, glancing at the front door.

He laughed. "You thought I was just going to take a few details and split like Sergeant Gerczak, right?"

"Yes," I said, thankful that he was the one to say that and not me. "That is all he did at the one last week."

"Where was that one?"

"It was over on Harrison Avenue, off Tidewater Drive."

"Nice area. I remember seeing that there was a report for vandalism there."

"Vandalism? That wasn't vandalism! Someone smashed in a window to a locked residence and trashed the inside. There was over eleven thousand dollars' worth of damage done to that property. How could that just be called vandalism?"

He shrugged, looking slightly uncomfortable. "I'm sorry, Ms. Young. I don't know the details or why it was listed that way. I'll have to pull the report and see what it says."

"I would appreciate it if you could. I'm pretty sure that breaking into a locked residence that you have no right to enter is considered burglary, even if nothing is taken."

He nodded as he grinned. "Yes, ma'am, indeed. Give me a minute to get my clipboard and notepad."

He turned and left the room as I stared at him. I should have filed a complaint on Sgt. Grumpy, but at least Officer Sexy—I mean Sexton—was taking his job seriously.

I took a couple of steps and peered around the wall to watch him walk out the door. I kind of had to agree with the nickname. He was rather sexy, but he was way too young for me. The officer was probably in his mid-twenties, and there was no way that was going to work for either of us.

Kayley, Book 5
When Kayley falls for a younger man, can she learn to accept her feelings, or will she lose something she didn't even know she wanted?

Kayley Young's life is about to undergo a few profound changes. Independent Kayley Young is a real estate agent in New York and loves her life as a single woman. She's not one to get tied down and leaves the baby-making to her siblings.

Officer Cameron Sexton is new on the job, a veteran of the military, and proud of his dedication to the job. Unfortunately, he finds himself annoyed at his lackadaisical sergeant, who should hang up his gun belt before getting someone hurt. When Cameron is dispatched to a burglary, he meets Kayley Young and is instantly attracted to her. Cameron has a feeling she reciprocates those feelings, except she's a little leery that he is ten years younger than her.

When Kayley's life starts taking a turn for the worst, she

depends more on the attractive young man she has let into her bed for fun than she intended. Her original thought of enjoying the moment starts to last longer, but Kayley's not sure that dating a man ten years her junior is wise for the long haul. Especially with the rest of the changes that have happened in her life. Can Kayley come to terms with the age difference, or will her family sway her away from the younger man?

ABOUT THE AUTHOR

Stacy Eaton began her writing career in October of 2010 and, as each year goes by, she releases more and more novels. Stacy recently took an early retirement from law enforcement after over fifteen years of service, with her last three in investigations and crime scene investigation.

Stacy resides in southeastern Pennsylvania with her husband, who works in law enforcement, and her two dogs. She has a daughter in college and a son who is currently serving in the United States Navy.

Be sure to visit www.stacyeaton.com for updates and more information on her books.

Sign up for all the latest information on Stacy's Newsletter!
Join my Newsletter and get TWO Short Stories for FREE!

STACY BOOKS - PAPERBACK

Rise Again Warrior Series

The *Rise Again Warrior Series* is an intense and emotional journey through the lives of many service members, their families, and their friends. Focusing on the trials that they face after wartime is over, and they have returned home to a nation that sometimes seems to have forgotten what they were fighting for, and what all of these people sacrificed in the name of Honor & Duty. Books Include: Mission: Believe, Mission:Accept, Mission: Repair, and Mission: Courage

Loving a Young Series

The *Loving a Young Series* is a steamy romance series that consists of six books. While these books are all standalone romances, the characters will be seen across the series since this is a small-town romance series about siblings finding forever loves.

Books include: Wesley, Henley, Riley, Kayley & Bradley

The Loving a Winston Series

The *Loving a Winston Series* is a five-book steamy romance series that spins off of the *Loving a Young Series*. Characters from both series will appear from book to book. Each book is a standalone romance with suspense and spicy romance scenes.

Books Include: Cara, Evan, Candy, Coral and Carmen.

The Unexpected Series

The *Unexpected Series* is a steamy romance series where anything can happen and probably will. Each book in the series is a stand-alone happily ever after, or happy for now book. While they are stand-alone, the books are all centered around Safety Zone Security and the employees there. Characters from one book will continue throughout the rest of the series. Books Include: Unexpected Packages,

Unexpected Arrivals, Unexpected Trouble, Unexpected Storms, Unexpected Desires, Unexpected Ties.

Paranormal Romance:

My Blood Runs Blue Series

My Blood Runs Blue Series is an adult Paranormal Action/Romance Series with vampires and is intended for mature audiences.

Books Include: My Blood Runs Blue, The Pulse of Blue Blood, Blue Blood for Life, Mixing the Blue Blood, Blue Bloods Final Destiny,

The Return of Blue Blood Series:

This series is 40 years in the future after My Blood Runs Blue. It is a very steamy series intended for mature audiences.

Books Included: Kristin: Blue Blood Returns, Hugh: Blue Blood Compelled, Zander: Blue Blood Reborn, Lena: Blue Blood Desired, Reckoning, Blue Blood Finale

The Twisted Love Series

(Dark Crime Suspense)

with Amy Manemann Co-Author

The Twisted Love Series is a continuing Saga of intense police procedures and romantic suspense and contains nine books in total. It delves deep into the world of crime and how it is investigated. Due to that fact, the crimes continue from one book to the next and could leave you hanging till the next one. Not all crimes are solved in the pages of one book. These books also contain strong adult language, violence, and sexual situations. Books Included: Love Lorn, Love Torn, Love Inked, Love Drowned, Love Carved, Love Trapped, Love Crossed, Love Twisted, Love Lies.

Single Titles

Whether I'll Live or Die

You're Not Alone

Garda ~ Welcome to the Realm

Liveon ~ No Evil

Second Shield

Distorted Loyalty

Six Days of Memories

Second Shield II: The Return

Tempt Me Too

Finding the Strength

Finding Love in Special Places:

Stacy's Short Story Series

Sweet Romance about adult topics. Stories include: Finding Love on Christmas Vacation, Finding Love on the Summer Surf, Finding Love with Dear Santa, Finding Love with a Champagne Toast, Finding Love on the High Seas, Finding Love on a Dude Ranch, Finding Love at the Farmer's Market

Heart of the Family Series

The *Heart of the Family* Series is a small-town steamy romance series that is best read in order. Books Include:

Mistletoe & Cocoa Kisses, Roses & Champagne Kisses, Orchids & Hurricane Kisses, Carnations & Hot Toddy Kisses,

Heal Me Series

Love Spicy Medical Romance? Check out the rest of the Heal Me Series for sexy romances that will warm your heart as they deal with life-altering medical and psychological issues. These books do contain language and open door sexual relations. While each book in the Heal Me Series is a stand-alone book, the characters cross between books and are best enjoyed by reading them in order. Books Include: Cured, Revived, Mended and Rescued.

The Celebration Series

The Celebration Series: Celebration Township is made for family, friends, falling in love, and don't forget celebrating the holidays. The first twelve books bring two people onto center stage as they overcome odds and figure out what their futures may hold. There is laughter, love, romance and even suspense when you join these couples as they each find a happily ever after over a holiday. The thirteenth book brings all twelve couples, and even a few special guests, into final focus as the first couple in Tangled in Tinsel prepares for their wedding one year after they met. Books Include: Tangled in Tinsel, Tears to Cheers, Heathens to Hearts, Rainbows Bring Riches, Sweet as Sugar, Making Mom Mad, Sparklers or Spankings, Raffles to Rattles, Flirting with Fireworks, Working Under Wheels, Masquerading at Midnight, Blessing & Beans, Velvet & Vows.

The Sometimes Series:

The Sometimes Series consists of three romances where the passion is a touch spicy and there is a hint of suspense is in the air. Sometimes You Win is a stand-alone story that ends with a Happy-for-Now ending. Sometimes you Lose, Book 2 of the series does end in a cliffhanger and Sometimes You Play the Game will finally give the couple a Happily Ever After. In all three books, you will find adult language and situations. Books Include: Sometimes You Win, Sometimes you Lose, Sometimes You Play The Game.

Pleasure Your Fantasies Series

The Pleasure Your Fantasies series is an ADULT Series with coarse language and intense sexual situations along with suspense. Books Include: Mistletoe Fantasies, Whispered Fantasies, Secret Fantasies, and more coming in 2024.

List Updated 9/6/23